Protecting HIS ASSETS

BAD BOY BOSSES

Protecting HIS ASSETS

BAD BOY BOSSES

J.K. COI

Entangled Publishing, LLC
10940 S Parker Rd
Suite 327
Parker, CO 80134
rights@entangledpublishing.com

Indulgence is an imprint of Entangled Publishing, LLC.

Edited by Kate Fall and Tracy Montoya
Cover design by LJ Anderson/Mayhem Cover Creations
Cover art from NewAfrica/DepositPhotos

Manufactured in the United States of America

First Edition December 2015

This book is for my mother and my sister, both strong women who would totally rock a pair of boxing gloves, but choose to be strong in other ways.
We don't say it often enough to each other, but I love you both.

Chapter One

"This is bullshit!" There weren't any appropriate words to describe what Steve Nolan was feeling right now...but that would do for starters.

He closed his hand into a fist on the thick oak desktop and glared at his business partner, Ben Harrison. "How am I supposed to get anything done with a babysitter dogging my every move?"

"Christ, Nolan. You're the one who made this course of action necessary. Maybe if you'd told me what was going on so I didn't get blindsided by emails from psychos, I would have given you the same consideration when I hired the security consultant." Harrison stopped pacing back and forth in front of Steve's office window long enough to level him with an expression of aggravation that managed to look simultaneously like heartburn.

Steve groaned and mentally talked himself down. The situation was making him crazy, and he hadn't meant to take it out on his friend...or the as-yet-unknown bodyguard Ben had hired without consulting him, who wasn't even here to defend himself. Yet.

"And just what the hell did you think was going to happen when I found out what's been going on?" Ben continued.

"Nothing," he said, still feeling stubborn, combative, and frustrated as hell. "Because it's none of your damn business."

"When it starts to affect Optimus Inc., you bet your ass it's my business."

Ben was right about that at least. Nolan sighed, stopping himself from dragging his hand through his hair. "Listen, I'm doing everything I can to find out who's behind this, but I'm handling it. The police didn't seem to think there was anything to worry about, so—"

"If you're so great at handling this, why did I have to call the cops? Why haven't you mentioned this before, done something about it sooner? Since when do you just shrug off a death threat?"

"Technically, it wasn't a death threat. More like... an expression of peevishness." In fact there'd been five of them. Five unsigned, undated notes slipped beneath his apartment doorway—and in one case, the door of a hotel room on the thirty-first floor of the Four Seasons. They may not have promised his death, but they'd threatened him with professional ruin and disfigurement of important personal appendages.

"Call it whatever the hell you want, but you aren't fooling anyone anymore. Real danger or not, this is already affecting our company and has to be taken seriously. That 'expression of peevishness' was leaked to the press, and if any more similar notes find their way there, our freshly released, brand new stock is going to plummet down to less than nothing before we even get the certificates printed." Ben glared. "And just for the record, the police didn't say there was nothing to worry about. They said they would look into it and that you should be careful."

Steve and Harrison had met through a common business associate and formed Optimus Inc. together. Nolan had the business savvy and public connections, while Harrison had the tech know-how. Their advanced machine-learning software specialized in AI analytics, and after a lot of work and an influx of capital from their new investors, they had finally released it three months ago to massive success.

"So I'll be careful, but I don't need a bodyguard," he said.

"It's a security consultant."

Steve snorted. "You can call it what you want, that doesn't change the fact that you're trying to saddle me with a babysitter."

"Too bad. I know you too well. Until we get some answers, this person sticks to you like glue."

Ben snapped his suit jacket and started for the door before Steve could voice another of his many objections. "The consultant has been recommended by the police department itself, and so you're going to facilitate."

In that case, the dude *must* be effective. He snorted. "Facilitate?"

"Damn right. It means you hand over those notes and cooperate while we figure out who's behind these threats. Understood?" His friend stopped with one hand on the doorknob and looked back at Steve with a fierce frown. "If you don't, I'll have no other choice but to bench you until the situation is under control."

"What is that supposed to mean?"

"If you can't cooperate with the police and your bodyguard, then you're a liability to this company. I can't have that, Nolan. *We* can't have that. Especially not right now."

"You can't be serious. This is as much my company as it is yours." But Harrison looked pretty damn serious. Shit.

"You seem to have forgotten we have stockholders now. It's their company, too. Do you really think I'll have any trouble voting you out if your problems threaten to cost them their investments?"

Steve was almost positive that Harrison wouldn't really do that, but the threat proved how seriously he was taking this.

"You're an asshole," Nolan muttered. But he was an asshole who was right, and Nolan was an asshole for stressing his partner out about it. "Fine. I won't fire the guy as long as he stays out of my way and doesn't draw attention to himself."

Harrison chuckled. "Don't worry, I have a feeling the consultant will fit right in with your image, and everything will appear to be business as usual while the police figure this thing out."

"The police aren't going to figure out shit, and you know it." He had no illusions about how investigations like this panned out. "But I agree with you that I shouldn't have ignored this for as long as I did. You know I would never put the company in jeopardy."

Harrison grunted. "I know that. And I understand why you didn't want me to know about this, but you would do the same thing in my place to protect me or the company. Which also means you're going to take care of this ASAP so Beth stops worrying about you. It's cramping our wedding plans."

Steve stifled a curse. Harrison and his fiancée were old business rivals who had reconnected at an industry event in the islands last year. Steve had kept this ridiculousness to himself specifically so his friends *wouldn't* worry about him when they were supposed to be planning a wedding and wallowing in their gooey, romantic happiness. That, and because he'd already been involved in enough drama to last him a couple lifetimes. This stalker crap would only drag that up in the tabloids again and get blown way out of proportion.

"You just can't stand that Beth likes me better than she likes you," he teased.

"You're right; she does like you. That must be why she named the new puppy Stevie." Ben chuckled as he opened the door. On the way out, he told someone waiting in the hall to "Go on in," and "Good luck."

Steve groaned inwardly, but he stood up and came around his desk.

A woman stepped inside his office stiffly, without smiling. There, she pulled up short and didn't move another muscle. She wore a stark black suit and sensible black shoes with short, square heels, and carried a slim leather briefcase in her hand. Her posture was stiffer than a board, and she looked him up and down as if examining a slug stuck to the bottom of her shoe.

He'd been expecting the bodyguard but was more than willing to put that particular meeting off for a few more minutes.

Besides being dark, it was impossible to tell what color the woman's hair was, pulled back in the tightest bun he'd ever seen. But the style showed off high, prominent cheekbones, and when she raised her chin, he was struck dumb by her brilliant blue eyes. Eyes that could drag a man out of the darkest hole and into the light.

He didn't know why she was in his office, but he was already making plans to take her somewhere more private and ruffle her up.

"Can I help you with something?" Had Kathy scheduled a meeting without letting him know?

"I'm here from the security agency..." God, her voice was all throaty. The stuff of midnight wet dreams. It made him instantly hard. "I'm the bodyguard."

The sweaty, naked images he'd conjured up careened to a halt like a thirty-car pileup on the expressway.

What? She was...*what?*

He wasn't sexist, and he had no doubt this woman was

good at her job or Harrison wouldn't have hired her, but…

"Seriously?"

"Do you have a problem with that?" She put one hand on her hip, but her smooth voice registered no surprise to his reaction.

He looked her over again, this time trying to focus on something other than the beckoning shape of her mouth, the graceful column of her neck, and the curve of her hip that was just perfect for his hands to hold on to. But no matter which way he turned, she still didn't look like the bodyguard type. If she lunged in front of him to take a bullet, she wouldn't even make a big enough target to keep him alive.

Not that he *wanted* her to take a bullet for him, of course, and it wasn't ever going to come to that.

"No, of course there's no problem. I guess I just expected a beefy dude with no neck wearing dark glasses, but you are much more my style." He gave her his most disarming smile, but her eyebrows only arched over those ocean-blue eyes with disdain.

He wondered at her reaction. Had they met before? Had he slept with her and forgotten to call the next day? He was usually very careful to keep his assignations entanglement-free, but misunderstandings had been known to happen no matter how upfront he was about his intentions.

"I believe your partner hired a woman because you're always surrounded by women, so nobody will think twice about my presence at your side."

Even though it was impossible to ignore the derision in the woman's purposely professional tone, Harrison was probably right. If Nolan had to have a bodyguard for a day or two, who better to have at his side than a beautiful woman? The tabloids were used to that, and it wouldn't even be worth the memory space to snap a photo.

"I suppose that's fair, but if you're going to fit the image, you might have to take off that ugly suit," he said, annoyed with her arrogant assumptions. By the pinched look on her face, she'd walked in here with her mind already made up about him, probably based on nothing more than the top five hits of a Google search.

She frowned and smoothed a hand over her jacket but didn't protest his assessment of her outfit. He'd thought for sure he would have gotten a rise out of her that time.

He walked forward and caught the faintest hint of cinnamon. Not enough to be overpowering. Just enough to make him think about tasting her. He shook off the thought and stuck out his hand, realizing he didn't know her name.

"I'm Steve Nolan, but I guess you figured that out."

"Good afternoon. I'm April Porter." Once again, her melodic voice wrapped around him like a velvet sheath, in sharp contrast to her austere appearance. It conjured unbidden images of darkened rooms and unmade beds. He self-consciously cleared his throat. She met him halfway and took his hand.

He was used to the clammy handshakes of his managers, all of whom seemed to bleed nervousness from every pore just being in the same room with their CEO, no matter what he did to put them at ease—although he tended to have much better luck with the women. But when Ms. Porter shifted her bag into the opposite hand and held out her arm, her palm was cool and dry, her grip strong. It proclaimed loud and clear that she would be difficult to intimidate, even more difficult to rile.

He couldn't help his curiosity. How did a woman who looked like a goddess become so rigid and controlled? He'd never been able to resist a challenge, and she was so very stiff and sober-looking, it was like a carrot dangling from a stick in front of him. He might not want a bodyguard, but he wouldn't mind the distraction of getting a woman like this to open up for him, like a juicy pineapple that was succulent and sweet once you got through the hard and prickly shell.

She clasped her hands over the handle of her bag and held it in front of her like a shield. This was a woman with something to prove, all right. The devil inside him was already aching to shake her up.

He waited for her to say something more, but nope, that was it. She looked as if she could stand there waiting patiently for an eternity. It made him vaguely uncomfortable. All that calm and stillness was unnatural, especially to someone whose longest stretch of inactivity was the four hours of sleep he crashed into every night.

Suddenly restless, he moved to the sidebar and opened the small refrigerator hidden behind a sleek mirrored panel. He and Harrison had finally been able to upgrade their offices just a few months ago, courtesy of a massively successful product launch, but now they needed another influx of investment capital to ramp production up to the next level. "Can I get you something? Water? Beer? Scotch?"

"It's twelve thirty in the afternoon." Ah, that voice. Despite the thread of disapproval, it was like warm caramelized sugar drizzling over his body—

"Then it's legal, right?"

"I'll pass, but thank you." Her lips pursed. She definitely disapproved. This might actually be interesting…and probably very wrong of him.

He shrugged and straightened again, moving to the big windows as he twisted the cap off the bottle of water and tipped it back for a long gulp. He watched her reflection in the glass, wondering when she would get impatient, but she only stood there…waiting.

He'd just met her, but there was something about her that had immediately rubbed him…not wrong, but…he wasn't sure. It felt like being in the cockpit of a jet and fighting the urge to punch it right into overdrive. He didn't know why or how, but just looking at her, standing there all subdued and calm, provoked him. He turned his back on the windows to face her again. "This job is a waste of your time and abilities," he said. "If you happened to want to hand in your resignation, I would make sure you still got paid."

She took a step forward, the look on her face telling him that she was clearly considering it. And why not? It was easy money for someone in her position. She could take it and still get another client before the end of the day.

He met her halfway until he towered over her and they stood only inches apart. "That doesn't mean we couldn't still see one another," he murmured, looking down at her pink lips and thinking about kissing her right here, right now. "Perhaps one night next week?"

With her head tipped back and that intensely direct gaze fixed on him, she lifted one slim brow, and his gut clenched with another hard stab of sexual awareness.

"That's pretty bold," she said, biting her lip suggestively.

He shrugged. "I don't like to waste time when I see something I want."

"And you want…me?" The rigid bodyguard persona had finally cracked, and her voice lowered to a delicious purr. His nostrils flared with triumph, letting him have more of her irresistible cinnamon scent.

"From the moment you walked in the door, baby," he admitted, lifting his hand to the back of her neck.

She shivered and her eyes fluttered, her body swaying closer so briefly it might just have been his imagination. A few baby-fine tendrils of her hair had come free and brushed his knuckles. He wanted to bury his fingers in her bun and tug her head back until her lips parted in protest and allowed him access to her mouth. Then they'd see how long she could hold on to her restraint and control.

"Even in this cheap, ugly suit?" she asked in a husky voice, running her finger down the lapel of her jacket and into the collar of her blouse, pulling it aside to show him the delicate edge of a pink lace bra.

Shit, she was screwing with him...and he deserved it.

He realized his mistake right away and let her go. She spun away and crossed the room. He'd gone in too hot when he should have played this one cool.

In his defense, it had been a while since he'd contemplated getting with someone outside of his social circles, where the women understood who they were dealing with and they wanted the same no-strings, no-expectations sex that he wanted.

She turned back to him with her arms crossed. "Why don't I stay for a little while?" Her voice was already cool and detached once more, but her eyes were still ablaze, and he had felt her reaction to his touch. She couldn't hide that from him now. "At least until I look at the threatening notes you've received and see what I can do about finding out who sent them."

"They're nothing," he said. "The police have a copy of the one that was emailed this morning, and they're looking into it now. I assume they'll track the IP address, find out the note was sent from the library or a cafe from a fake account, and that will be the end of it."

"And if it's not?"

"Then they'll flounder around, pretend to chase non-existent leads for a few more weeks, and the entire incident will go into a neatly labeled file folder until someone gets tired of it being there in the cabinet a year from now and throws it away."

"The file wouldn't get thrown away. Left unsolved, it would be stored in—"

"Not the point," he said, annoyed.

She cocked her head as if she were trying to pull him apart and find out what made him tick. Was she now realizing she couldn't just rely on Google for all her information about her new client? "You don't have a lot of confidence in the police's ability, do you?"

"Is there any reason why I should?"

She shrugged. "I guess that's why I'm here."

"And what do you think you can do that they cannot?"

"We'll see, won't we?" A hint of a smile tugged at her full mouth, making his cock throb and his brain go *there* again. Just like that he was picturing those lips wet and bruised from a blistering kiss, parted in passion. Even without any makeup, her lips were a tempting pink. Not to mention exceptionally full and lush, despite her pinched reserve and stiff regard.

He liked confidence in a woman. And intelligence. And apparently he liked sass, all wrapped up in a straight-laced, tight-lipped bodyguard.

Damn, but he wanted her even more after that little tease than he had before.

He wanted to find out what made *her* tick. He wanted to make good use of that mouth as he was exploring every inch of her creamy skin, breaking her calm facade and uncovering all of her mysteries. But he'd learned his lesson, and he would be more subtle.

"In the meantime, I think I should stay close to you to ensure your safety," she finished.

"All right, if you want to waste your time following me around, who am I to complain?"

"Thank you." Her tone softened, and his breath caught when she unexpectedly smiled. "I know this was not your decision, and I'm grateful you're taking it so well."

"Save that thought until after you hear my conditions for your continued service."

Her smile froze. "Conditions?" He returned to his desk

and sat down, leaning back in the oversized leather chair and knitting his fingers behind his head as he looked up at her. When she didn't follow his lead, he held out his arm and motioned for her to sit as well.

He took it as a good sign when her shoulders relaxed slightly and she placed the briefcase on the floor beside her and lowered herself into the chair. When she crossed her legs and tugged the hem of her skirt to her knees, he couldn't help but watch. And when she bent over to pull a slim notebook from the depths of the bag and the front of her blouse gaped just enough to give him another shadowy glimpse of that fragile pink lace against her smooth, creamy skin, he felt like a seventeen-year-old boy again.

If he had any faith that a bodyguard—male or female— could actually be effective, he might have considered hiring Ms. Porter to watch over his mother and sister, just in case this threatened to touch them. He accepted that he would be stuck with her for a day or two to appease Ben and keep the shareholders from becoming alarmed. That said, if anyone found out that *he* had a bodyguard, it would only fuel rumors and gossip and create the kind of media circus that Optimus Inc. desperately needed to avoid now. If she couldn't blend in, this wasn't going to work.

"If word gets out that I hired security, it'll be all over the internet in seconds. The email that got copied to the press has already started tongues wagging, and our shareholders are concerned. Any more drama could make them lose confidence in Optimus Inc. Whoever is doing this, they can't be allowed to believe that they've succeeded in scaring me. I won't let *anyone* ruin what Harrison and I have worked so hard to build."

She frowned. "I think everyone would agree that your safety is more important than your public image, and your company should be able to withstand a—"

"If my safety were actually in peril, then sure, whatever you say. But that has yet to be confirmed, and right now..." It was a critical time for the company. Any more signs that there might be trouble could affect how the next few days played out. "I'm taking zero risks. We are *not* going to find out what my company can withstand. Got it?"

She nodded. "If that's the way you want it. Then what are your conditions?"

He could still fire her, to hell with Harrison. But what would be the fun in that?

"I'll allow you to conduct an investigation in whatever way you see fit, as long as it's discreet, and as long as you run all of your findings through me before you talk to anyone else," he said.

She nodded immediately. "Understood."

"Good. And when it comes to the bodyguard thing, we're doing it my way, despite what Mr. Harrison may have told you."

She opened her mouth. "In my experience, a client doesn't always know what's best for his own safe—"

"*This* client does." He shut her down before she could finish. "So if you want to keep this position and you insist on tagging along after me, you are going to have to remain completely inconspicuous." He looked her up and down with a critical eye. "That means dressing like the type of woman I would be seen out in public with."

He hadn't meant that the way it came out.

Ms. Porter was a drop-dead gorgeous woman that any guy would kill to be seen with. She could be dressed in a burlap sack, and it wouldn't matter. But this was about business, and if she stuck to him like glue in that ugly suit, combined with her rigid posture and stoic expression, it would be as effective as an ad in the paper announcing that there was blood in the water at Optimus Inc.

But her lips had pursed in reaction to his words, and at last another hint of emotion lit up those impossibly blue eyes. Even if it was only irritation…it would do for starters, so he didn't bother to correct himself.

"It also means that *none* of this becomes fodder for the news hounds," he continued. "In fact, I want you to sign an NDA. I'll have my assistant draw it up."

"A non-disclosure agreement? I don't really believe that will be necess—"

"Well, I do. The only person who knows about your purpose for being here besides myself is my partner. So if I so much as hear a whisper in the media about Steve Nolan needing a bodyguard, I'll know where it came from, and it'll be your ass on the line."

She frowned. "I would never—"

"Don't bother to tell me what you'd never do," he snapped, swallowing the bitter taste of remembered betrayal. "I've heard that one before."

She paused, her gaze assessing. He tapped his fingers on the desk.

"All right," she said finally. "I agree to your conditions."

"Good."

Let the games begin.

Chapter Two

"Then we have a deal, Ms. Porter?"

April allowed a crisp nod as she swiftly rose to her feet, giving in to the crazy compulsion to be on an even playing field with the inimitable Steve Nolan. She needed to be right there at eye level—although technically his eye level was about seven or eight inches higher than hers.

"We do, Mr. Nolan. As long as you keep up *your* end."

She stifled a wince at the words *your end*. Had she really said that? Had it sounded as suggestive as it did on her tongue, or was she self-conscious because he had hit on her within moments of meeting her...and she'd liked it?

You've met high-powered, handsome men before.

You've met high-powered, devastatingly *handsome, compelling men before.*

Oh, who the hell was she kidding? She'd never met a man like him. A man who looked even better in person than he did on the cover of *GQ*. With sunshine in the gold flecks in his eyes and charisma bleeding from his pores, even when he was obviously frustrated by a difficult situation.

Exactly the kind of guy she stayed away from as a rule.

He held out his hand, the curve of a smile on his lips. "Shall we shake on it?" Steve Nolan was way out of her league.

Fifteen minutes ago when she'd walked into this office, she'd already known it. The proof was in the bulky designer watch on his wrist, and the cut of his custom suit. It had been there when he'd looked her over in her cheap clothes and mentally dressed her in something that wouldn't embarrass him in his social circles.

He was just like Jeremy.

That fact should make it easy to do her job, collect her money, and then pretend that he'd never existed.

She glanced down at his outstretched arm. He waited.

Yes. It should be easy.

She gave in and his fingers closed firmly over hers. There was a leashed strength in his grip typical of the kind of men she'd been around all her life. It represented the type of power that didn't come from corporate position or social standing, but was purely physical.

When he drew back and smiled again, she tensed, suspicious of his smiles more than his frowns. Like the last smile he'd laid on her, it felt like a weapon instead of a simple expression, designed to make her vulnerable, to trick her into letting down her guard and exposing her true self.

That's ridiculous. You're just the hired help. You'll be lucky if he remembers your name tomorrow morning.

He was going to be one of those clients who didn't take her seriously. He wouldn't take the situation seriously, or the fact that it was her job to protect him no matter how ridiculous he believed that job to be. From the looks of him and what she knew of his reputation, he didn't take much of anything seriously.

It should have been enough to turn her off, but she couldn't calm her racing heart, and she couldn't stop thinking about the warmth in his fingers when he'd touched her. She shouldn't have let him talk to her that way, should have put a stop to it before he'd gotten so close. When she'd realized that he was actually blatantly hitting on his bodyguard of *five minutes*, some perverse, wicked part of her had wanted to turn the tables on him, and so she'd played along.

Well, the tables had been turned all right. Her skin still tingled, and her lungs felt too full.

She told herself that she had experience dealing with his type. Intimate experience. Her ex Jeremy had taught her the hard way that there would always be a wall between people like her and people like them, and it was best not to cross it.

So she squared her shoulders and shored up her defenses. She would be the most professional security consultant she could be. She needed the money this contract would bring in to pay for her father's cancer treatment and wasn't about to lose the job because her client was a playboy.

"Can you show me the letters now, please?" she asked, eager to do something to change the focus of both their attention.

He extended his arm in an invitation for her to sit again. She picked up her notebook and flipped it open.

"The only letter I have here is the one that Harrison received by email this morning, and that has already been forwarded to you," he said.

Yes, she'd seen a copy. *Cut the bastard Nolan loose, or see your company fall into hell right along with him.*

"As far as warnings go, it's less specific than those that were addressed to me personally, but no less hostile."

"Why didn't you do anything about them before now?"

"Honestly, I couldn't be bothered. Personal attacks are nothing new after years in the media spotlight." He paused and frowned. "But attacking my friends or my company... that's another matter altogether, and to tell the truth, if

Harrison hadn't called the police first, I might have done so myself this time."

"And you don't know why the media received a copy of the email?"

"I assume the bastard wasn't satisfied with my lack of response after his first few notes, and this was an attempt to make me believe he's serious," he replied in a dry tone. "And maybe also to lay the groundwork for a monetary demand. That's usually the next step, right? First you scare the victim with threats, then you demand money in exchange for making it all go away?"

"If that is, in fact, what this is all about," she agreed. "If the incident escalates to that point, the monetary demand is probably going to be paired with a more specific threat. For example, the perpetrator may promise to reveal some secret that could damage your reputation and affect your business if the money isn't paid. Is there something out there that could be used against you?"

He laughed. "What could be worse than what's already out there?"

There'd been a scandal involving his family a number of years ago. She'd looked it up briefly after getting the call from her boss, Nora, this morning about the job.

Starting way back in the mid-1920s, Nolan's family had started a manufacturing company. It had weathered the changing marketplace well over the years, and it had become the leading manufacturer of internet-based software in the eastern United States. But then Robert Nolan, Jr., Steve's father, assumed control of the company, and a few years later, he killed himself when it came out that his CFO had robbed the company blind.

"The other notes were on paper, made from pasted magazine cut-out letters, like the guy watches too many cop shows. So the media didn't get copies of all those, just the one sent by email to my partner this morning. But I can't afford for this asshole to stir up any more trouble."

"So where are the other notes, then?" she prompted.

"In my office at home," he admitted. "I threw out the first one thinking it was a bad joke meant for someone else, but when I got another one I started keeping them. I got the last one two nights ago. It was waiting for me outside the hotel room door of a...uh...woman friend, and I found it when I was leaving for the night."

Feeling the heat climb up into her cheeks, she frowned down at her notepad. "That's not good. It would imply that—"

"I know what it implies," he said with a scowl. "It means this bastard has been following me around and watching my movements, as well as sending his cowardly little notes."

She nodded. "All right, we should get those as soon as possible. Are you available to leave now?"

If she could get her hands on the notes, there was a chance she could run them over to the police station and have them analyzed before the end of the day, which might even turn up a set of prints and put this case to bed before she would have to spend an entire night with Steve Nolan.

No! Not *with* him. Watching over him. *Over* him.

"No. After the fiasco this morning with the email and the police, I have a thousand things needing my attention, so I'll be here for a while," he said.

He wouldn't appreciate being told that his safety might be more important. It was obvious that even after admitting someone had been spying on him, he still didn't believe he was in any actual danger. At this point, she was willing to concede that he might even be right. This was looking like a typical annoyance case. Still, her job wasn't to make assumptions, and so she needed all the information.

"I understand. Whenever you're ready, let me know. I suppose tomorrow will be soon enough for us to take the notes down to the police station and find out what they can come up with."

"Us?" He raised a brow. "As fun as an 'us' might be any other time, going to the cop shop is not on my agenda."

"You really don't like the police, do you?" She tilted her head. "Do you want to tell me why?"

His jaw clenched. "Let's just say I would rather solve this matter on my own."

"And yet, you haven't," she pointed out drily.

"Only because it isn't worth my time. Whatever this asshole thinks he's going to accomplish, he's dead wrong. I know how to deal with trolls and bullies, and I refuse to give the fucking son of a bitch the satisfaction of intruding on my life, or thinking he can get to me with these pathetic scare tactics."

A chuckle slipped out before she could stop it. "After so many years in the public eye, do you really have zero filter on that mouth of yours?"

He barked out a genuine laugh, too. "None whatsoever," he admitted with a grin.

His eyes sparkled with vitality and a natural charm, just like they did in all those magazine photos of him going out on the town with beautiful women—a different one every time. Her gut clenched. She would have bet money on that sparkle being just a trick of the camera lens, but the reality of Steve Nolan was so much more compelling than she could ever have prepared herself for.

She cleared her throat and squeezed down on her reaction, trying not to think about the way those eyes might sparkle if he had her naked under him in bed. "I'm a little surprised you haven't required the services of a bodyguard sooner."

His grin faded. "Listen, there's been no actual violence committed against me or anyone else. After the email this morning, I think this is probably an amateur attempt at corporate sabotage by a competitor who would like to see Optimus Inc. fail. If that's the case, I agree that we need to find out who's behind it as soon as possible. Otherwise, even though the notes have gotten pesky, they're not death threats or anything, and I have no intention of changing my life around because of it."

After a long moment, she nodded. "All right. I won't ask you to alter your schedule...yet," she added sharply. If he didn't fall in line, she'd be asking for that and more. "At this point, I only request that you share your complete schedule with me—both daytime and, er, nighttime activities—so I can accommodate you in the safest way possible."

She cleared her throat and felt another blush bloom across her skin after she said *nighttime.* Nolan nodded toward the door. "I have work to do. You can get what you need from my secretary, and I promise not to leave the office until after five o'clock. I assume you also have something else you can be doing until then."

She gritted her teeth at the summary dismissal. Yep, he was going to be one of *those* clients. She didn't think his attitude was about her. So far, despite the impertinent flirting, he hadn't been disrespectful about her ability to do this job, not like some guys would have been. He just couldn't seem to respect the danger that he might be in. "I'm sorry, but I believe it's best if I remain at your side," she reminded him tightly. "Even here."

"I should probably be safe enough in my own office with the door closed, don't you think?" He gave her a little smirk. "Or do you want to come over here and make sure no one's hiding under the desk?"

He obviously got a kick out of pushing people's buttons, so she didn't give him the irritated reaction he was probably hoping for. Instead, she glanced around the room with a clinical eye.

Honestly, he was absolutely right. Nothing was going to happen to him here. He was alone, and she could monitor his visitors from the reception area. "I'll be right outside."

"I can get you access to the office next door. It's likely to be more comfortable than sitting in my waiting room."

She shook her head. "Thank you, but I'll need to vet everyone who comes and goes throughout the day."

He sighed and shook his head, but he didn't object, which surprised her. "Suit yourself," he said. "Let Kathy know if you need anything, and she'll make sure you get it."

April made her way to the door but glanced over her shoulder as she pulled it closed behind her. The vaguely annoyed, cavalier rascal was gone, and he seemed suddenly weary. He'd closed his eyes and rubbed the back of his neck.

She looked away quickly and left.

True to his word, Nolan didn't come out all afternoon. Through the door, she heard him talking, though. Nonstop. For someone rumored by some to be nothing but "the pretty face" of Optimus Inc., the man certainly had a lot of work to do.

Not long after she left the room, a mechanical noise started up from the other side of the office doors, but when she jumped out of her chair to check it out, Kathy laughed and stopped her.

"Treadmill," she said with a grin and a shake of her head. "I swear the man has ants in his pants. He can't sit still long enough to compose an email." As she lifted her headphones, she said, "Which is why I end up having to listen to hours of dictation to do all his typing for him."

Reluctantly, April sat back down and listened to his running steps hitting the track without pause for an impressive hour and a half. Even during that, the soft rumble of his voice never stopped. She imagined him dictating instructions to his secretary, or maybe talking into a Bluetooth at his ear, all while running, or pacing the floor, or doing push-ups, or whatever else he had room for in there. The uncomfortable ache from sitting in the chair in his reception area all afternoon settled deeper into her own bones.

She passed the time trying *not* to call her dad. He'd told her this morning in no uncertain terms to keep her distance while he was getting another round of radiation treatments this week. He'd said he didn't want her to see him "like that," and no matter how much she'd objected that she should be there to help him through it, he'd refused to allow it—which was another reason she'd taken this assignment. She needed to stay busy, or she'd start crying…and might not be able to stop.

So she listened to Kathy tapping away at her keyboard and reviewed the notes she'd made so far, starting with her research into her client's past. There'd been a lot of coverage in the papers ten years ago about Nolan Sr.'s death. She'd been in high school then, but the story had been big, and local, and everywhere.

The CFO who'd stolen from Nolan's company, Jason Fielding, had fled to Colombia. Then all evidence pointed to him dying in a car crash two years later, although the fire had burned up any trace of a body, and there'd been no sign of the stolen money.

The no body thing set off alarm bells for her. April pulled out her cell to call a friend at the Bureau. She explained the reason for her interest in the case and was told that someone matching Fielding's description had recently been flagged entering the National Bank in Bogota and accessing a safety deposit box registered under what they believed to be an assumed name. So far, there wasn't enough evidence to warrant seizing the contents, but they were keeping a close eye on the area. "Does that mean Fielding isn't dead?" she asked.

"Sorry, but all I can say is that the agency has resumed an active investigation of the case."

She thanked Charlie for his help and said good-bye, but he quickly added, "Hey, when are you coming back to the program?"

She winced. He had been her mentor in the FBI training program, and while he'd been supportive of her need to leave so she could take care of her father when he got sick, he never let her forget that time was ticking by. "Things are still up in the air right now, Charlie."

"Your dad's doing better, though, right?"

She wished she could say that everything was fine, and she'd be back at the FBI next month...but it wasn't going to happen, and she'd known when she made this decision that it would probably be the end of her career as an agent.

She thanked Charlie again and hung up as soon as she could, wondering if Steve Nolan knew about the development in his father's case, or if he even cared now, ten years after the scandal.

It must have been horrible at the time. The family had lost everything. The company. Their ancestral home. Their money and social positon. The life they led now would still be considered privileged by normal people's standards, but it wasn't even close to the kind of life Nolan's wife and family had been accustomed to when Robert was alive, although Nolan had been successfully making up for it on his own.

He'd still gone to NYU on a football scholarship. In fact, somehow, amid a flurry of episodes involving too much drinking, too many parties, and a ton of women, he had managed to graduate at the top of his class a year earlier than all his classmates. He had become the media's Cinderella story: a gorgeous guy from one of America's oldest and richest families stuck in the ash and dust of his former life who'd clawed his way back to the top.

"You're seriously still here?" April looked up to find him staring down at her. His hair was ruffled and damp from a shower, and he hadn't bothered to put the tie back on. It was almost impossible to process just how good he looked with one hand in his pocket and one shirt button undone. She resisted the urge to smooth her skirt over her thighs and pat her hair. Maybe a skirt hadn't been the most practical decision, but her boss had assured her she wouldn't need to chase anyone down today, and she should go for the inconspicuous look while she had to be with the CEO in his office for the day.

He adjusted the briefcase in his other hand. "Did you sit there all day?" He sounded as if that would have been akin to torture.

She bit her cheek to hold in her response. Patience was a learned attribute that didn't come naturally for her, but the FBI training had been good for that.

He didn't wait for her to answer but turned to his secretary with another one of those smiles he seemed to share so freely with everyone, even though there was more strain in his eyes than there'd been earlier. "You shouldn't be here either, Kathy. It's after six."

April tucked her tablet into her bag and stood. Was six late for him? With his reputation for partying, she couldn't see him being one of those who put in regular nine-to-five hours.

The woman looked at her watch and tsked. "If you hadn't come out of there just now, I would have stomped in and dragged you out. Revener can wait until Monday you know."

Was Revener a company? A product? That reminded April that she wanted to address his earlier remark about corporate sabotage. If she was going to investigate the threats against him properly, she would need access to the deals Optimus Inc. might be negotiating and get a list of their corporate competitors.

"Get out of here, and I'll see you next week," he said.

"Your mother called twice this afternoon," Kathy said as she grabbed her purse.

Nolan blinked and turned his back on April. In a lower voice, he asked his assistant a question. She couldn't hear it, but she understood once Kathy answered him, since she didn't modulate her response as he had done.

"What do you think she wanted? She asked what your calendar was like for the next two weeks." Karen grinned and Nolan scowled. "If she's setting you up again, at least warn me so I'm prepared for the angry phone calls from strange women when you forget your date and stand them up."

Did he do that often? Forget his dates? What else might he have forgotten? Who might he have snubbed badly enough to want revenge? She filed the possibility away for further contemplation later.

Nolan didn't defend himself, but he wasn't happy. Because his mother was setting him up? Or because his assistant had spoken out of turn? Why would he care? It wasn't as if she wasn't already aware that he was one of the biggest players in the city.

She had to haul ass to keep up with him as he strolled out of the office to the elevators.

"What was that about?" she asked. He jabbed the button hard and they waited.

"What was what about?"

"You know. Back there with your assistant. You were upset when she told you about the phone call from your mother." She didn't think that Steve Nolan's own mother was stalking him, but she couldn't know for sure what information might or might not be relevant to the investigation, so she had to ask questions about everything.

Two guys in suits came down the hall toward them, slowing as they also got to the elevator. "It's none of your business."

She frowned. "Do you and your mother have—"

He quickly leaned in close, eyes flashing. "Stop right there," he interrupted in a clipped voice. "Kathy knows better than to talk about my personal life. And if you want to keep this job for more than five minutes, you will also learn that lesson right here, right now."

Her mouth dropped open. She wouldn't have thought that the guy whose grinning photo ended up in headlines on a weekly basis would get so prickly about his privacy. Then again, if her picture was being snapped every time she went out in public, she'd probably put on a brave face about it and then let loose with the frustration behind closed doors, too.

"I apologize. I shouldn't have intruded." Her voice dropped to a whisper as the two men stopped behind them to wait for the elevator. "But that was still harsh."

The moment lengthened beyond his annoyance, beyond her contract, beyond their differences. His gaze remained intent and direct, focused on her. A stab of awareness hit April's core, and his eyes flared as if he knew it…right before he put his devil-may-care playboy face back on.

He straightened away from her and grinned at the associates who'd joined them, asking after their day. She took a deep breath and looked up. Her throat tightened as the floors marking the position of the elevator ticked higher and higher. This morning, she'd ridden in it, but then it had been empty.

The door slid open on a glass enclosure full of people ready to head home for the day.

It wasn't empty now.

She tensed. It wasn't the height or the idea of putting her life into the hands of a mechanical coffin that bothered her— although she tried not to think about that too closely, either. It was having to stand next to upward of fifteen other people, all of whom were breathing their germs into the confined space, that threatened to make her throat close.

But they were on the second-to-top floor of a fifty-story building, and there wasn't any other reasonable way of getting to the bottom, so with a deep breath, she forced her leaden feet forward and crossed the threshold first. She held the door for Nolan with her elbow and then stepped back beside him. She kept her hands off the railing and talked herself out of holding her breath. It was too long a ride for that.

She looked over and found him watching her, a smidgeon of curiosity in his eyes.

She felt the need to say "I'm fine," but didn't, and not even because he hadn't asked. In fact, he'd already turned away to answer a question from another occupant.

It wasn't lost on her that hers wasn't a normal reaction, but with every one of her father's chemo and radiation treatments, his immune system got weaker, and she'd gotten more paranoid. She couldn't help but worry about him contracting an infection that he couldn't fight off, all because she'd ridden in a germ-infested elevator, or shaken someone's hand.

You're losing it. She *needed* to be able to do this job. Not only for herself, but for her father, too. She'd been told in no uncertain terms just last week that contrary to his expectations, the medical insurance would not cover all of the bills that were piling up.

She tried to focus on faces. You never knew when or where you would see a face again and what it might mean. But nobody stood out as not belonging. Even the bike courier at the seventh floor smiled and waved at someone before squeezing inside, obviously in the building often enough to develop a rapport with some of the employees.

Two women dressed almost identically in black blazers and pencil skirts chatted together. One of them was older, maybe sixty, with sleek blonde hair and a few thin lines around her eyes.

The other woman was in her thirties, with bouncy chestnut hair to her shoulders. Her posture stiffened, and she cast an annoyed look over her shoulder as the guy standing too closely beside her laughed at something his friend said and carelessly nudged her arm.

The two men talking to Nolan had already loosened their ties for the day. One of them swept a hand through his slightly greasy hair before reaching for the hand rail. April winced. Both of the guys seemed to get more relaxed with every ping of the elevator as the floors counted down, and they decided which bar to hit up for a drink.

The elevator stopped, squeezing everyone closer as more passengers entered. The woman who'd been annoyed with a brush against her arm was now plastered right up against the same man, and April squeezed herself into the corner. She was very aware of the brush of Nolan's shoulder against hers, and the rumble of his voice as he made conversation. The cadence of his words imprinted deep in the pit of her stomach and the subtle scent of the soap still fresh on his skin invaded her lungs.

When they reached the first parking level, Nolan put his hand over the door and waited for her to step out, but she hesitated. "My car is here," he said.

"Mine is on P3." The visitors' level. She didn't usually bring her car into the city. It was impractical to drive downtown, but she hadn't known what to expect and had to be prepared to follow her client anywhere.

"It looks like you've got a dilemma then." His eyes gleamed with amusement. He was having a lot of fun baiting her, and maybe she should be offended, but it was easy to understand why all the women fell at his feet. She could see why every magazine and newspaper wanted to find an excuse to put his picture on their cover.

He was hot, but so what? Lots of guys were hot.

Except there was way more to it than that. He was more than just a pretty face with a bright future, and there was nothing like a devastatingly gorgeous guy with power and money, whose smile lit up…everything.

Her breath caught. He knew exactly the effect he had on people, and she had no doubt that he used their expectations against them, used his reputation as a smoke screen, used smiles and subtlety to put people off balance.

She thought she understood a little better what she was dealing with, and she wasn't going to be that girl again—the girl who gets starry-eyed by the charm and attention and forgets to wonder why a gorgeous guy with power and position would bother with someone like her.

Because the answer was never the right answer, and the charm and attention was just a game…one that was rigged.

Yes, she knew better.

He was still holding the door, watching her. She slipped out of the elevator without even touching him, but her skin still tingled and her breathing hitched. Too bad knowing didn't seem to be making any difference. He'd apparently decided he wanted to get under her skin…and it was certainly working. She would have to shore-up her defenses if she was going to make it through this job.

"Will you come with me in my car in order to adhere to the letter of your assignment, or will you be a rebel and just meet me at the gym?"

"The gym?" She frowned. "I thought you were heading home. I would prefer it if you returned home at this time. I can protect you much easier in the safety of a private space, and I still need to get the other anonymous notes from you as well."

"I need to work out," he answered with a careless shrug, making it clear that making her job easier was not one of his priorities.

"Didn't you already spend a ridiculous amount of time on that treadmill this afternoon?"

"That was just to keep me from clawing at the walls. I don't react well to prolonged periods of inactivity." His voice lowered an octave, making it clear just what kind of activity he preferred most.

"You could meet me at my apartment later if you'd prefer, and I would be more than happy to hand over the notes then."

"You know I can't do that. Until you're tucked safely in bed for the night, I stick to you like glue."

"That should be fun." He waggled his eyebrows. It was such a goofy thing to do, she struggled not to laugh. This wasn't a date. This was a job.

She might be fairly new to the bodyguard business, but she'd been trained to expect victims of this type of personal invasion to be frustrated and scared, which usually translated into misdirected anger or paranoid hermit behavior. Either Steve Nolan was exceedingly adaptable, or he was no stranger to unwanted attention, and none of this even fazed him. Probably a combination of both.

"How long do you plan to be at the gym?" she asked.

"It depends how I feel."

Did the man even know what a schedule was?

"Don't worry." He raised his right hand, palm out. "I promise to go straight to the gym without passing Go, and I won't even cross the street unless you're there to hold my hand."

His posture shifted, and there was a subtle tension in it. Beyond all the jokes and the wantonly unprofessional sexual advances, he wasn't as indifferent about all this as he pretended. He was pissed about having to answer to her, just better at hiding it than most, so she tried not to bristle beneath his teasing condescension.

"I'm just trying to do my job," she reminded him gently. "And I'm *not* your mother."

His jaw clenched, and she held her breath as his gaze narrowed and slid over her body. Slowly, casually, purposefully. A visceral perusal that left her buzzing from head to toe. He could have used his hands and it wouldn't have felt any more intimate.

"No, you're definitely not," he finally said with a cocky, lazy smile. "I wouldn't make that kind of mistake."

He was purposely trying to make her uncomfortable, to test her limits. It was all just a game to him, one that he was used to winning, but she'd played that game before and lost, and it wouldn't happen again.

The arrogant curve of his lips made her whole body tremble.

Okay, so she might consider playing…but she knew the rules now, and nobody would be taking her heart as the prize.

She squared her shoulders and stepped away from the door. "Where is your gym? Wait for me outside the garage, and I'll follow you there."

"Park Place, between Church and Broadway."

She swore under her breath. "The boxing club?"

"You know it?" He sounded surprised, but she wasn't in the mood to indulge his curiosity. She simply nodded and turned back to the stairwell.

"Oh, and Ms. Porter?" She glanced over her shoulder with raised brows. "I suggest you wait outside, or dress appropriately."

"I can't wait outside. However, I'll stay out of your way. I'll be fine as I am."

"Didn't you hear what I said earlier?" His imperious tone plucked at her temper.

"I heard you." Her hand clenched on the stair railing. "But I don't understand how my attire affects my ability to do this job."

"If you stand around a place like that dressed in your ugly suit, you'll stick out like a sore thumb, and we agreed that you would be completely inconspicuous, did we not?"

She bristled, forcing herself not to look down at her jacket and skirt. She was getting tired of him calling it ugly. It wasn't a pencil skirt and stiletto heels, but her suit was clean, presentable, it fit properly, and it let her do her job.

"I have workout clothes in my car," she bit out.

Chapter Three

The club was busy, but Steve and his buddy Leo had a standing reservation, and after a few minutes at the speed bag, their ring opened up. He looked around and frowned when he couldn't find his sparring partner.

Leo Markham was a society divorce lawyer by day and boxed semi-pro the rest of the time. Steve didn't know how he explained the bruises to his high-class clients, although the guy rarely had to worry about bruises. He was a rock-solid wall of Italian muscle that could go round after round and dealt more hits than he ever took.

As Steve adjusted his gloves, his gaze alternated between the double door entrance to the gym and the door of the women's locker room on the other side of the large athletic facility. He'd signed in his new shadow as a guest, although he hadn't seen her yet.

For someone who took her job so seriously, she hadn't seemed eager to come to the boxing club. She was probably pissed because he'd refused to run home and hide behind his apartment door with the shades drawn. But until some real danger had been established—and he didn't think that was going to happen—he wasn't about to change his life around.

He didn't see that black suit of hers, which was a good sign. But then, where was she? Had she called her boss already and asked them to send someone else? She hadn't seemed the type to give in so easily, and he liked that about her. Maybe too much.

He grabbed his water bottle and took a big gulp, his gaze lighting on a woman coming out of the locker room.

This April Porter was nothing like the straight-laced, restrained professional who'd waited patiently in the uncomfortable chairs outside his office all afternoon. This woman was a fucking Amazon dressed in body-hugging Lycra, showing off a sleekly toned, athletic body designed to make men weep.

Holy shit, the difference a pair of shorts and a sports bra could make. He'd already suspected what lay beneath her ugly suit, but the reality made his mouth go dry, and it was sexy as hell.

She was immediately approached by Big Joey—the owner of the club—and her guarded expression transformed into a warm smile that lit up her entire face and sent Steve reeling with a fresh wave of desire. Surprisingly, it seemed they knew each other. Big Joey touched her shoulder, and suddenly her smile faded and sadness filled her eyes. He frowned and started forward, but she saw him and her shoulders went back like a soldier at attention, confirming Steve's suspicion that she was only so formal with him. It didn't matter. He couldn't take his eyes off her, and by the hint of pink in her cheeks, she'd noticed.

She nodded to Joey and made her way over. "Are you already finished with your workout?" she asked.

Frustrated, he shook his head. "I was hoping to get into the ring, but it looks like it's not going to happen. My sparring partner didn't show up." After a day spent thinking way too much about his prickly, intriguing new bodyguard, his body had needed the physical release of an intense, all-out fight.

She bit her lip and looked around the gym. Finally, she groaned and said, "I could spar with you."

He raised a brow. "You know how to box?" She wasn't wearing the proper shoes, and she hadn't carried out a pair of gloves with her from the locker room.

"My dad was a fighter," she said, looking as if it physically hurt to open up to him even that much.

"That doesn't mean *you* can fight," he said, egging her on.

"Try me," she answered.

The challenge in her words hit him at multiple levels. Oh, he wanted to.

"All right. Then let's go." He caught the hesitant eagerness lighting up her eyes. Finally, he'd found something that could break through her icy shell. If only *he* had the same effect on her.

He reached down for a pair of rental gloves from the bin by the ring. "Are you okay with these?"

She nodded and put one on. She wrapped tape around her wrist with a practiced hand, and he knew she wasn't just blowing smoke up his ass; she owned a pair of her own. When she tucked the second glove under her arm and slipped her hand inside, he reached for the tape and grabbed her wrist. She was very still while he held her, and he found himself lingering so that he could touch her longer than was necessary.

When they climbed up into the ring, she alternated stretching her arms over her head and behind her neck and danced on the balls of her feet.

He went through the motions, too, but he'd already warmed up, so he was really just watching her.

A few minutes later, she nodded and moved to the middle of the canvas. "Ready."

She threw the first punch. He cut back and turned to follow her as she slipped off to the left, but when he countered, he held back, and she had no trouble dancing out of reach. "What was that? I've seen children punch better than that," she taunted him.

He grinned. "All right, you asked for it."

His next shot landed true, but she shrugged it off and followed it up with a wide bolo punch. He blocked and responded quickly with a combo counterattack to the ribs which she deflected by catching him in the chin.

He was surprised by how good she was. Her stance was perfect and relaxed, her reaction time was quick. She knew how to judge her opponent's next move and beat him to the punch. She knew when to take a shot and when to hold back and wait for a better opening. He marveled at the strength in her small bones. She was a natural, and before he knew it, both of them were breathing heavily. The cool, controlled Ms. Porter he'd met earlier today had melted away with the sweat of their exertion. There was a smile on her face—and that was maybe the biggest surprise. Her smile did things to him that should be banned out of the bedroom. It was like a lightning bolt to his gut.

He spat his mouth guard into his glove and grinned. "You've got moves, Ms. Porter."

The color in her cheeks deepened beyond what could be blamed on the physical exertion, sending a bolt of lust through him so strong he wanted to tell everyone else in the gym to go to hell and throw her down on the mats.

She grunted and held her fists up in front of her face, but Steve had already gotten the workout he came for, and his body was now intensely focused on its other needs. He'd been guiding the fight just so he could watch her chest rise and fall when she danced away, and so that he could brush up against her as often as possible.

She took a rash, reckless swing at him, the kind of swing she never would have taken at the beginning of the fight. Was he wearing her down? And not just physically?

His grin widened, and he sidestepped. She doubled back, but tripped over her foot when he feinted, throwing her off balance and right into his arms.

Like a charm. She smelled like cinnamon even with the sweat beading her skin. Her breathing hitched as she tilted her face up, and those pouty full lips were right there, begging for the pressure of his mouth, the tug of his teeth. His forearm curled around her small waist, pulling her tighter to his body and taking her weight. She didn't pull away, her gaze dipping down, down, to the spot where her Lycra-covered breasts pressed against his bare chest.

"Oh God," she whispered, then jerked her gaze up to his in horror as if she hadn't meant to say it out loud.

"What the hell was that?" someone yelled from the sidelines.

Big Joey.

Ms. Porter closed her eyes and stiffened. She shoved against him, but he was slow to release her. The club owner climbed into the ring and stalked toward them with smoke practically coming out of his ears. He looked like a monstrous bull next to her slim, catlike form, but she didn't shy away from him.

Steve quashed the crazy impulse to step between them, frowning. Even knowing this woman for less than a day, he was certain she wouldn't appreciate his interference.

"Your da would crucify you if he saw what you just did, dropping your guard in front of your opponent like a rank amateur." Her gaze slid sideways back to Steve for a fraction of a second, long enough for him to see the regret pulling her face back into its stern, professional mask.

She slapped at his hand with her glove and stretched her

neck out to the left and right. "Cut it out, Uncle Joe. We were just sparring." She looked over her shoulder at the crowd that had gathered to watch their match and groaned.

Uncle Joe?

The club owner snorted and dropped his hands to plant both fists on his hips. "Don't you talk to me as if I didn't halfway raise you. Now…" He spun around and glared at the gawkers. "What's everyone looking at?"

The men began to disperse. Big Joey turned back around and frowned. "By the way, April honey, you never did say what you're doing here. I take it you're with *this* guy?" He jerked a thumb at Steve with a sneer.

"Just doing my—" she started, then sputtered as she remembered that she couldn't tell anyone that she was on a job. "Well, actually I'm…uh…"

Steve stepped in. "We met last night, and April here promised to give me some pointers in the ring," he said, suggesting that they'd met on *very* personal terms. Beside him, she winced, but true to her word not to let anyone know her real purpose for being with him, she didn't contradict him even to someone who was obviously a friend.

Big Joey frowned and crossed his arms. Her lips pressed together in a thin line. The engaged light that had glowed in her eyes during their sparring match had faded. In fact, the air around her was cooling by the second, as if she was mentally putting on her ugly suit again, distancing herself.

He was lost as to why. After seeing the way she'd brightened in the ring—from a utility bulb into a freaking strobe light—he honestly had no idea what April Porter was all about. She was a dichotomy, but one he ached to decode.

Big Joey looked Steve up and down, but there were no jokes about his getting boxing pointers from a girl. "Well, there's nobody better than April Porter… Just as good as her da, she is."

Steve glanced at her. Was his bodyguard blushing? "I suppose I can't disagree with that," he said, although he had no idea who her father was, except that he'd been a fighter.

She cleared her throat and gave Steve a properly contained smile. "Thanks for the sparring match. If you're finished your workout, I'll change now and be ready to go in ten minutes. Please don't leave the gym without me."

Her voice dripped with that professional stiffness, but he nodded. She turned away and ducked beneath the ropes, jumping down out of the ring. She unwound the tapes on her gloves like a pro and peeled them off, then dumped them on the bench and made her way to the locker room.

Damn, she could bounce quarters off that tight ass.

Beside him Big Joey cleared his throat. "What do you think you're doing with that girl, Nolan?"

Steve had been a member of the boxing club for three years, but he'd never been on the receiving end of a look from Joey quite like the one he was getting now—a look full of warning and protectiveness.

He raised an eyebrow. "It's just like she told you. We're just hanging out for a while," he said. "Then again, if I *was* doing something, I'd be doing it with a mature, adult woman who knows her own mind and makes her own decisions... don't you agree?"

Big Joey leaned close and spoke softly. "Listen up then. I've known her since she was a kid running around this gym. April's been through enough from guys like you. If you do anything to hurt her..."

Interesting. He never would have pictured Big Joey as the type to make threats, but he sure was protective of Steve's new bodyguard. "From what I just saw, I think she can probably take care of herself," he said with a shrug.

"Just keep what I said in mind."

Fifteen minutes later, Steve came back onto the floor, hair

still damp from a quick shower. The gym had quieted down a bit, and Ms. Porter waited just outside the men's locker room door. She was once again dressed in her suit. Her gym bag was thrown over her shoulder, and she stood beside one of the structural posts as if she had all the time in the world. It was hard to tell which had more steel in its posture; her or the post. The only evidence that anything at all had changed since they'd left the office was the fact that her hair now hung down to her shoulder blades in a thick, damp ponytail instead of rolled up on top of her head.

Standing like that, dressed like that, she was definitely *Ms. Porter* again. Steve could find no sign of a boxing spitfire named April with the world's most amazing smile.

She stepped forward. "Are you ready to go home?"

He shook his head. "Actually, no. I have dinner plans," he said.

Her lips thinned as she narrowed her gaze, but he wasn't intentionally trying to be difficult...this time. With all the distractions today, he'd forgotten he had a date until the reminder had popped up on his phone while he'd been changing. He checked his watch. There should be just enough time to make it to the restaurant.

April pulled up to the curb across the street from the classy restaurant and watched Nolan get out of his car and hand his keys to the valet. Before he proceeded inside, he actually looked her way. She could swear he was even making eye contact through her car window.

Not only was she not dressed for dinner at the fanciest restaurant in New York, joining him inside would be oodles more awkwardness in one evening than she'd signed up for.

She was surprised he'd even bothered looking for her car.

The few other clients she'd protected had quickly gotten used to her presence and simply accepted that she was always there somewhere. Otherwise, they'd forgotten about her until they needed something. She was like a statue and hadn't warranted human interaction unless it was absolutely necessary.

Before they'd left Big Joey's, she'd asked for the name of the restaurant. There'd be no way to remain inconspicuous at a table by herself, especially dressed as she was and especially if she didn't order something. Staying outside in the car had been a calculated decision, but he'd promised to text "911" to her number—which she'd programed into his phone back at the gym—if absolutely anything looked suspicious. She'd written down his license plate number and would make a point of checking over the car when he came back out to retrieve it from the valet, but for now there was nothing to do but wait…and think.

It had been a mistake to follow him into the boxing club. She'd known it would be virtually impossible to go unrecognized at Big Joey's, and her dad would probably find out about it before the end of the night—even from his hospital bed. But the bigger mistake had been offering to join Nolan in the ring. It had felt *amazing* to put on a pair of gloves, and before she'd known it, she had almost completely forgotten who he was supposed to be to her. *Just a job.*

She looked at the digital time glowing from the dashboard and sighed. It wasn't so bad being a bodyguard. The pay was decent, and she was good at it. If only she weren't so distracted by the subject of this particular assignment.

Steve Nolan.

The way he'd looked in a pair of loose-fitting gym shorts and boxing gloves, the promise of sex in every pull and flex of muscle, had made her mouth go bone dry and kicked the attraction she'd been fighting since the moment she walked into his office into high gear.

She'd put on the gloves as an excuse to keep from standing there drooling over him, watching all those muscles rolling and bunching and tensing, but with her body humming from the physical exertion, loaded with adrenaline, begging her to give it another outlet, she hadn't stood a chance.

Your reaction had nothing to do with the fight.

It was *still* begging for release, and she couldn't get him out of her head. The whole package. Corporate suit guy and hot athletic guy had merged into one irresistible guy so that now, even with his clothes back on, it was impossible not to notice that he'd been blessed by the gods of broad shoulders and tight asses. Or that his hair had a stubborn kink in the front that looked devilish, but had to drive him batty. Or that there was so much energy buzzing off him, he was like a live wire threatening to shock her every time he came within a foot of her.

It was heady stuff, making her aware of him in a way that made her aware of herself in a way that she hadn't been aware of in a long time.

If that made any sense at all.

Don't acknowledge it. Stay professional. Letting herself think of Steve Nolan as anything other than a responsibility would be disastrous. Jeremy had lived in his same world, and for a while, he had been her dream come true. Good-looking and charming. Passionate and attentive. Smart and full of ambition. She was dizzy with love right up until the moment it all came crashing down. The moment she'd overheard him telling a big group of his buddies at a party he'd taken her to at the country club that he was just slumming it for a while before settling down with someone connected, glamorous, and worthy of being the future governor's wife. There hadn't even been one among them who'd disagreed with him. Every one of those guys had nodded and clapped him on the back like it was the only thing to do.

After that, there'd been no doubt in her mind what guys like him were really all about. Princes who came along and fell in love with girls who'd grown up in a rundown gym that smelled of sweat socks and stale air didn't exist. Since Joey had taken it over from her dad, he'd cashed in on the upswing in the sport's popularity. He'd put in all the best equipment and started charging an arm and a leg to new members, but when all was said and done it was still just a gym.

She swore and closed her eyes, leaning over and briefly bashing her forehead against the steering wheel. The hard-molded, rubbery scent made her nostrils flare, but it didn't distract her nearly enough. She might have had better luck getting Steve Nolan out of her head if she hadn't enjoyed herself with him so much. His laughter and his energy made her shiver with anticipation. The heat in his eyes when he looked at her was enough to melt her resolve down to nothing. It was a fight to hold on to it.

She checked the clock for the third time. It was closing on eleven. She glanced out the window and finally saw the valet bringing Nolan's Mercedes back around, so she got out of her car and jogged across the street. She pulled up just short of the curb just as he was exiting the restaurant with a tall, drop-dead gorgeous redhead clinging to his arm, but a honk from the Cadillac behind her reminded her she was still in the road, and she dashed ahead with an apologetic wave over her shoulder.

He nodded to April as she approached the car, but as his date turned and curved her lithe body into his and whispered in his ear, his attention shifted. He smiled and whispered back, his hand around her waist. April sucked in a breath as if she could feel that hand hot on her own waist.

She shook her head and refocused with a swallow. She conducted a visual inspection of his car, ignoring the twisting of her stomach, blaming it on the fact that she'd missed dinner to sit outside and wait two-and-a-half hours for him to be finished with his.

She performed her walk around in such a way that only Nolan himself might have noticed what she was doing. Anyone else would think she was just waiting for her own car, or maybe waiting for her date to show up. Friday night near the theatre district meant there was enough of a crowd for her to go virtually unnoticed, so he shouldn't have any complaints about her being too conspicuous.

Another car pulled up behind Nolan's, and the valet got out to hand the keys over to the redhead. Nolan took her arm and walked her around to the driver's side, opening the door like a gentleman. The woman slid into the leather seat in such a way that her bosom almost fell out of the low-cut dress and the slit in her already short skirt spread to show off more of her crazy long legs. Flaunt 'em if you got 'em, she supposed.

She'd reached for the knot of Nolan's tie and tugged until he bent closer to her. He looked a little stiff and impatient now, but a sexy smile twisted his lips as he put his forearm on the roof of the woman's car. If he hadn't, she might have actually pulled him all the way inside the vehicle on top of her.

April shook her head. There was no reason why she should feel this weighted disappointment perched on her chest like a giant ball of indigestion.

The woman's fist curled around Nolan's tie, and his mouth was almost touching hers when a flash of light caught the two of them mid lean-in.

April spun around in time to see a scruffy-looking guy with a big pot belly in a ratty old golf shirt holding up a heavy camera with a massive zoom lens. Instinctively, she stepped in front of the photographer to block the next shot. The flash went off, and the guy swore. He was going to get an impressive photograph of her chin. April feigned confusion like she had no idea what just happened.

The photographer shot her an annoyed look and angled around her before lifting his camera for another picture. This time April knew she had to try something more direct. She took a deep breath and plastered a big smile on her face. She pretended surprise and squealed loud enough for everyone to hear, jumping in front of him again. Startled, the man faltered and frowned.

"Oh my God." She waved her hands excitedly. "That's a huge lens on that camera. I just *love* cameras. I'm always taking pics of my cat and putting them up on Instagram. Do you have Instagram? Hey, lemme see." She reached for his arm to pull the camera closer as if to try and get a look at the screen and find out what he'd been photographing.

He jerked it out of her reach nervously like he was afraid she might break it and took a step back. Nolan just stood there watching the scene she was making. A real smile pulled at the corners of his mouth, the kind of smile that every paparazzi would kill to get a shot of, and his eyes twinkled with it. She felt her breath vacate in a rush and her legs went weak.

Damn, she was in some serious trouble if she couldn't even handle his smile without melting into a puddle in the street.

His date, on the other hand, didn't look so amused. The expression on her face was made up of mostly annoyance, mixed with a smattering of impatience.

April was trying her best to respect his wishes not to let *anyone* know that she was his bodyguard, but if the photographer came any closer, it would be more difficult to prevent him from getting his photos without becoming obviously physical, and that would definitely let the cat out of the bag.

Two men in suits exited the restaurant. One of the valets went to them and pointed to her and the camera guy.

The two bouncers—did fancy restaurants call them bouncers?—approached with purposeful strides, and the photographer's face fell. He knew he'd been outed, and he quickly slipped back into the shadows without getting too pushy.

Stopping in front of her, one of the restaurant's bouncer-porter dudes looked down his nose at her, probably taking in her "ugly" suit and deciding that she was the problem. *One of these things is not like the other*. It was plain as day that she didn't belong there with all the slick, richly dressed society types.

"Can we help you with something, miss?" he asked in a deep, heavy Brooklyn accent. "A taxi cab, perhaps?"

Nolan stepped up and tapped him on the shoulder, a deep frown pulling his expression tight. She shook her head to warn him off. She'd managed to keep her purpose from becoming public knowledge this long. There was no point in letting him blow her cover now just because the porter was being rude.

She smiled widely. "I'm just waiting for my date. We got separated coming out of the show. I'm sure he'll be here in a minute."

When the other porter nudged him in the arm and nodded to a figure standing a few feet away with his cell phone held out to take a picture—it was a completely different guy, and thankfully the phone wouldn't be able to zoom in close enough to do any real damage—they left her alone and stomped over to hassle him. She let out a low breath of relief.

Nolan was already being tugged back by his date to her car. She pulled his head down with a siren smile.

April barely refrained from gagging.

"Are you sure you won't reconsider?" the woman murmured in a husky voice after kissing him in a completely inappropriate-for-public-viewing sort of way. Hadn't she seen the paparazzi? Or didn't she care? Or maybe she *wanted* to be in the papers and saw Nolan as her ticket to stardom.

April turned and cleared her throat as unobtrusively as she could, but if he and Jessica Rabbit there didn't get out of the valet line soon, they were going to attract more than just paparazzi, and April would resent having to protect him and his slutty girlfriend from a restaurant full of angry people who only wanted to get their cars and go home.

She squared her shoulders, praying for a break in the after-dinner traffic so she could run back across the street to her own vehicle. She kept her gaze low, but could just imagine the look of invitation shining from the beautiful woman's eyes, and she silently groaned. Was she going to have to follow Steve Nolan out on a booty call? Sit in her car on the curb outside this woman's apartment while he was inside screwing her?

She shook the horrendous image out of her head. Oh Lord. Her previous assignments hadn't prepared her for that kind of situation. Her first assignment had been as part of a small security detail to the twelve-year-old daughter of a politician in Connecticut during campaign time. She'd protected a semi-famous female pop singer who had received a few unwanted love notes from a rabid fan. And she'd agreed to accompany an overly paranoid elderly lady who hadn't been in any danger at all but wanted someone to drive her across the country to visit her daughter's family because she'd hated to fly.

She grinned to herself. Nolan was already looking for any excuse to get rid of his bodyguard. She probably shouldn't mention those fluffy assignments, or he'd start to doubt her qualifications.

Suddenly, she realized that he was looking right at *her*, trying to straighten away from the redhead, who wasn't giving in that easily and pulled him back to her again.

"I'm sorry, I can't tonight," he said to the woman in a low

voice, "but I'm glad we could meet for dinner. I'll call you."

I'll call you. April winced. No specifics. *And that*, April wanted to tell her, *is what's called "the brush-off."*

Finally, he left his date—without kissing her again—to return to his own car. As April turned with him, she noticed a slim woman with a black silk scarf tied up over her dark hair giving him a dirty look, probably for holding up the valet line for so long, but he either didn't notice or he was arrogant enough not to care. There was something vaguely familiar about the woman, and April glanced back for a second look, but the bystander had already disappeared into the shadows of the growing crowd.

April darted out into the street, sprinting to avoid an oncoming taxi cab. She yanked open her car door and slid into the driver's seat.

"Please let him just go home," she muttered. "Alone." This kind of thing was not what she'd signed up for when this job had come her way, although she probably should have expected it when she found out who her assignment was.

All she wanted now was to get the anonymous letters and make sure he was safely behind a locked door for the night, so she could call in the overnight backup, go back to Dad's empty house, and inhale a bucket of ice cream. She felt a flash of anxiety because it would be too late to call the hospital and check on him, but she'd called earlier and he'd been asleep. The doctors had her number if anything happened.

When Nolan pulled out from the curb, April followed. Thankfully, the redhead's vehicle did not.

Even better, Nolan headed straight for his apartment, but as they neared the driveway she quickly realized she wasn't going to be able to trail him all the way into the parking garage under the building. There was a card reader posted at the entrance, and she didn't have a pass.

It was good to know there was some security in the

building, but she would have to get a pass in the morning so next time she could proceed into the garage as well. Since there was nothing to be done about it immediately, she circled the block once and then was lucky enough to grab a spot on the curb around the corner as someone else was leaving. She left the car there while she went inside to the lobby.

"Good evening, miss." The doorman was a beefy guy without a neck who looked uncomfortable in his uniform jacket, but he had a wide smile and super bright teeth that had seen one too many whitening strips. "Who are you visiting, please?"

A door opened across the hall. It was Nolan, coming in from the garage. She was relieved but surprised. She'd expected him to forget about her altogether, or at least take the elevator right to his apartment and force her to get the doorman to call up for permission to let her follow.

"Good evening, Mr. Nolan."

"Hi Doug, how's it going?" he said with a friendly smile before coming over and sliding his arm around April's waist to pull her close. "The lady's with me tonight, okay?"

It was barely a real touch, but her belly clenched, and her heart started to race. She edged back as unobtrusively as she could manage even as the scent of him beckoned her closer.

He was evil, and they were going to have a discussion about just how far he was allowed to go to maintain his dictate that her true reason for being with him stay a secret.

Doug nodded without pause and turned back to her. "Do you want to give me your keys, ma'am? I can bring your car into the garage for the night. If you leave it out there on the street, you'll have a ticket in the morning."

She quickly shook her head. "I'm only staying a short time, Doug. But thank you." His eyes widened as she realized what that might have sounded like. "Oh Lord," she stammered, feeling her cheeks heat. Beside her, Nolan chuckled out loud without an ounce of shame.

"I only meant that I'm here to pick up some, um, paperwork from Mr. Nolan and won't be long. We're business acquaintances, nothing more."

At this time of night? Could she have come up with a worse excuse? Now he thought she was a prostitute *for sure*. It didn't help that Nolan was grinning from ear to ear, having way too much fun making April uncomfortable, or that his little display of fake affection just a minute ago had already put ideas into the doorman's head.

But to his credit, Doug kept his cool. "My apologies, ma'am. Of course. I'll keep an eye on your vehicle until you're ready to leave."

"Ah, nothing to apologize for. Thank you," she said, pinning Nolan with a glare. He only smiled back at her evilly. "I'm sure Mr. Nolan appreciates that you take such good care of his guests."

Nolan stuffed his hands in his pockets, completely casual. "Doug's the best. Nobody gets past him."

They said good night, and Nolan turned back around to the elevator. *Another elevator.* "What floor do you live on?" she asked.

He looked sideways at her as the door started to slide open. "The twentieth." He moved to step inside.

She reached for his arm to hold him back until she'd had a chance to make sure the elevator car was empty and had to bite her lip to keep from letting out a surprised hiss at the unexpected shock of touching him. Even through the suit jacket he was warm, thick, hard.

He looked down at her hand on his arm. She yanked it back quickly. "Sorry."

She started to tug the front of her suit jacket before stopping herself. Fiddling with clothing was a classic indicator of nervousness. She should know, she'd been trained to read all the signs. Even if Steve Nolan did make her nervous…hot and breathless and nervous…she was determined to at least *look* professional.

She nodded and stepped in after him. At least it was empty but for the two of them. Before the door closed, she took a deep breath. There were germs everywhere, yes. But ever since her dad had gotten sick, she'd become more aware of enclosed public places like this as concentrated pockets of disease. It was irrational, but she couldn't seem to help it.

When he reached out to press the button for the twentieth floor, she couldn't look away. How many other people had touched that button today? Yesterday? The day before? How could he be sure that the cleaning service had disinfected the keypad? Or *when* they'd last disinfected the keypad. Or that they even cleaned any part of the elevators at all? How could he be sure that the last couple to come in together after a romantic dinner hadn't decided to get the private part of their evening started early? Leaving the issue of cleanliness aside, it was amazing how many people didn't even care that there were almost always cameras in elevators.

She looked up and realized she'd been watching the elevator buttons with too much intensity, and now he was watching her curiously. "I'm sorry, did you say something?"

His expression hadn't changed, so maybe she wasn't being as obvious in her freak-out as she thought she was.

"Thank you for what you did back at the restaurant."

She shrugged, relieved. "I didn't do anything." Only her job.

"You handled that photographer"—he said the word with the kind of derision that came from more than just a cursory experience with the breed—"much better than I would have. If he'd tried to take one more picture, I would have decked him, and that would only have gotten me in more hot water with our investors when the news hit the Net."

"You wouldn't have hit him." She was pretty sure about that. "You've never hit any of them in all the years they've been hounding you."

His gaze narrowed. "And you know this, how?"

"It was a long afternoon. I did some research and called a friend at the FBI."

"And do bodyguards usually have connections with the FBI?"

She didn't answer, but she thought a lot of them probably did, or at least they had connections with the police. She knew from experience that personal protection was the fallback for cops and agents when that career path became closed to them, for whatever reason.

"What else did they tell you?"

"Nothing." She didn't want to mention what she'd learned about Justin Fielding's Colombian accounts just yet. It might not be related to her assignment at all, and she didn't want to overstep the bounds of her contract by admitting she'd dug up dirt she had no business digging up. Since the FBI seemed to be keeping an eye on the embezzlement case, if there were any developments, the agents should be the ones to approach Nolan about them, not her.

"So, your father is a boxer?" he asked, changing the subject again.

The question made her frown. Where had that come from? What did it matter? "Was," she clarified. "He *was* a boxer. Now he's retired." *And dying of cancer.* She swallowed hard.

"That sounds like it could have been an interesting childhood." When his lips twisted up like that, she just wanted to take one between her teeth and —

"Not really." She shouldn't talk to her client about her personal life. Even if Nolan wasn't technically asking about *her*.

"And how long were *you* a professional boxer?"

Okay, scratch that. She glanced at him sharply. "Me? What makes you think I was a boxer?"

"You certainly seem to know your way around the ring."

She shrugged. "I grew up in that world, so yeah, I learned a few things along the way, I guess. It's good exercise, too. But that doesn't make me a professional."

Would Nolan analyze her words and realize that she hadn't actually come right out and denied anything? Not that it was a big deal. She'd boxed for the IFBA for three years to make enough cash to get through college. She'd been good at it and could have stuck with it, but her father had practically forced her out the first—and only—time she'd come home with a fractured cheekbone. He'd always wanted her to have a career that would last her a lifetime, one that wouldn't break her spirit along with her bones. He'd been so proud when she graduated with honors and made it into the FBI training program.

She shook off thoughts of her father that would only make her melancholy. Nolan looked contemplative. She'd tried to remain focused and impersonal with him, but it seemed she lost a little more of that resolve every time he spoke to her. Was he taking all the small pieces of information that she'd dropped throughout the day and working out where they fit in the puzzle that was April Porter?

She wanted to tell him to stop it. There wasn't really anything interesting about her anyway. She shouldn't rate high enough on the social scale for him to bother trying to figure her out. There were way more interesting women out there. Women who belonged in his world. Women who didn't work for him.

"Well, you looked good up there," he finally said, "like you were enjoying yourself." His voice lowered in appreciation, insinuating that he'd noticed more than just her boxing stance or her smile.

Damn it. There were undercurrents in that deep drawl that she couldn't possibly afford to acknowledge, and it was more than the filterless, inappropriate teasing she figured was his standard operating procedure.

She looked down at her feet, marking the floors by the musical *ding* and counting down until they would be out of the elevator, and she could put more distance between them. Her thick-soled, utilitarian boots looked ridiculous next to his shiny black leather designer shoes. He needed to look down at them, too, and be reminded of how ridiculous the two of them would be together.

"Your girlfriend is very pretty." As a change of subject, it was pretty lame and decidedly obvious. She winced and rushed to add, "I'll have to get her name. What does she do?"

"Jennifer isn't… We've been out a few times, but it's not serious."

Really? After the way they'd acted together outside the restaurant, his idea of serious must be different than hers. On the other hand, the woman had been the bolder of the two of them. Surprisingly, he hadn't taken advantage of her blatant invitations and had even managed to send her home alone without seeming to cause any disappointment or hurt feelings.

"And you are *not* running a check on her," he finished.

April said nothing. She didn't need his permission to do her job. And her job was protecting him, even when he thought it was a joke. She'd get the information she required one way or another.

"Don't think you can go behind my back, either." His voice was suddenly sharp and cold as ice. "Or you'll be out on your ass so fast, you won't know what hit you."

She snapped her gaze up to his with a gasp, surprised that he'd figured out exactly what she was thinking. "You can't do that."

"Watch me." His tense jaw seemed carved from stone, and she was startled to realize that she'd mostly bought into that laid-back, playboy act he'd been trotting out all day.

For a second, she had peeked behind his easy-going, approachable CEO face. Just for a second, but it was long enough to confirm that there was definitely more to Steve Nolan than the public got to see. She suspected there was more to him than even most of his friends got to see.

Her shoulders stiffened. At one time, she might have been intrigued and drawn in by those sharp glimpses of intensity, by the hint of danger. But that was a more naive April from a different time. She was no longer interested in guys like that...she wasn't. Besides, with her father's illness, she didn't have time for intense romantic entanglements anyway.

She curbed her tone. "I am diligently trying to do my job here, Mr. Nolan. But if you insist on curtailing this investigation and putting unreasonable limits on my duties, it's only going to take longer to get to the bottom of this." She shrugged as if it was no skin off her back. "That's fine because I get paid by the hour no matter how long it takes, but I was under the impression that time was not on *your* side."

He ignored her and pressed forward, crowding her backward until the handrail along the wall of the elevator bisected her spine. She schooled her features. His face was inches from hers, so close she could see the brilliant flecks of gold in his deep brown eyes.

She realized it was one thing to tell herself she wasn't interested, quite another to mean it. Especially when Nolan was looking right at her—*into her*—as if he could see and feel the pounding of her pulse. Especially when he still smelled of a fresh shower, which reminded her of the sweat that had poured down his chest back at the gym. Especially when she hadn't had sex in *so long,* and his exact brand of strength, confidence, and magnetism was her drug of choice—notwithstanding that it was a drug that would only add complications to her life that she wasn't equipped to handle.

"Whoever's playing these sick games is a stranger," he murmured darkly. "It isn't anyone close to me, so you do not need to interrogate my friends."

"How can you be so certain?"

"Because no one who knows me at all would dare fuck with me like this." He smiled, but this time he didn't try to hide the dangerous predator lurking behind the perfectly cut suit and stiff silk tie. He was a sleek, powerful shark whipping silently through the dark water. And as his gaze flicked to her mouth, she knew he'd set his sights on *her* as an appetizer.

It wasn't hard to imagine what he would do to someone who betrayed him, but she also knew from personal experience that no matter how safe you thought you were, the pain of betrayal could come from anywhere. The people closest to you were often the ones who ended up hurting you the most...whether they meant to or not.

She gritted her teeth. The air between them thickened as they stared one another down. "The reality is that in cases like this, nine times out of ten the perpetrator *is* someone who—"

"No."

The finality in his voice dared her to contradict him again, but she wasn't about to start that kind of argument in an elevator. If he wanted to wear blinders when it came to this investigation, then she wouldn't push it for now. There were plenty of other rabbit holes to explore. She hoped for his sake that he was right, but if the time came when all the other leads turned up empty, and the only ones left were the ones Nolan didn't want to acknowledge, then they'd have to do things her way.

Suddenly, his fingers touched her cheek. She gasped and leaned back, but there was nowhere for her to go unless she bolted to the other side of the elevator, and showing fear to a predator was always a bad idea.

His head dipped. "You might have a bruise there tomorrow," he murmured with a frown. He'd caught her in the chin during their sparring session.

She cleared her throat, flustered by his about-face. "I'll be fine. You barely touched me." She put her hand over his, but he only shifted his touch to the slope of her neck, leaving goose bumps in his wake. She shivered all the way down to her belly and bit her lip to stifle a groan. Her stomach and thighs clenched and her fingers curled into the sleeve of his jacket. She hadn't even realized she'd dropped her hand to his forearm but she couldn't pull away, even though she knew she should.

His eyes darkened, all that intensity narrowing on her until she couldn't breathe. *Dangerous. This is stupid and dangerous, and you're only going to regret—*

And then he was kissing her, and it was nothing like what she'd imagined, not that she would ever admit she'd been imagining it at all; at least not more than once a minute since he'd stripped down to his gym shorts and boxing gloves, dripping sweat and oozing testosterone. Blood, laced with adrenaline and lust, pumped through her veins as hard as if she'd spent hours in the ring.

He didn't fall on her like she was a prize he would claim, and he didn't swoop in, trying to catch her off guard. His kiss was testing and calculating, just like him. Telling her exactly what he wanted and daring her to be bold enough to admit she wanted it, too.

She couldn't admit something like that. Not even with her heart hammering like a speed bag at full tilt.

A groan escaped her lips, and he took that as permission, deepening the kiss. It should have bothered her, made her uncomfortable and nervous, but for once she was consumed by something stronger than self-preservation, the fear of losing her job, or the worry that had plagued her the last several months.

The elevator dinged, and she felt the drag as it pulled to a stop and the door started to open. She heard something, a distinct *click* out in the hallway, and jerked her gaze up over his shoulder, worried that they had company, but there was no one there.

He leaned back in like they had all the time in the world. His hand cupped the back of her neck, the other planted flat against the wall beside her shoulder, but the only other part of him touching her was his mouth. God, his *mouth*. His mouth consumed her, devoured her, took control of her until she almost whimpered with defeat.

Stop. This has to stop. She twisted away with a gasp, even though she couldn't quite make her fingers unclench from his arm.

Thankfully, he immediately backed off.

Crap. She was such a freaking hypocrite. Hadn't she just been thinking how irresponsible it would be to get carried away in an elevator? Hadn't she spent the evening telling herself to stay focused and professional?

"You fucking jerk," she snapped, angry. So angry. But with him…or herself for being such a stupid, weak glutton for punishment? "You were kissing another woman *less than an hour ago*."

She shoved him, both hands slamming him hard in the chest. He leaned back, but his feet didn't move. And then he smiled. The bastard actually *smiled*. "She was kissing me, actually," he said, as if it made a difference.

"What? And you thought that since you couldn't go home with her, I would just stand in like it was a part of my job description?"

He stood in front of her, not touching but not retreating, either. "Let's make one thing clear." The elevator door was closing on them again, but Nolan didn't move. "When I kiss you, it has nothing to do with your job."

She snorted and shoved her hand into the crack of an opening before the door closed all the way. "You assume it's going to happen again."

"I don't make assumptions," he corrected her. "I calculate inevitabilities."

Chapter Four

As they finally exited the elevator, Steve noticed the door to the stairwell swinging closed. Had someone wanted to take the elevator and been scared off by the horny couple making out inside it?

He probably shouldn't have kissed her. That could bite him in the ass in a thousand and one different ways. But he couldn't regret it, especially not after getting such a hard-fought reaction out of her. Both reactions. First, her delicious submission, and then the beautiful outrage. The truth was, he'd do it again. In a heartbeat. In fact, he'd been looking for a reason to kiss her all day, and the impulse had little to do with tension or stress. It had everything to do with her. And him. The two of them being impulsive and sweaty together.

That sounded like him, all right. Too bad it didn't sound much like the very proper Ms. Porter.

During dinner with Jennifer—who was the perfect combination of shallow and self-involved so that he never felt guilty for holding his real self back—"Ms. Porter" had been all he could think of. She had vaguely disquieted him with her unshakable reserve and unnatural stiffness, but she'd also intrigued him. She was interesting, competent, and mysterious. And then she'd become an Amazon at the gym. She'd punched his imagination into high gear, sending crazy, sweaty fantasies streaming through his brain.

Both sides of April Porter that he'd already seen fascinated him so much that he'd been less interested in taking his warm and willing date home, and unreasonably eager to spend just another five minutes with his new bodyguard. He was more than a little curious about the other sides she might have.

Even so, by the time the elevator door slid all the way open, Steve knew he'd miscalculated. The kiss had been too much, too soon. Walking beside him now, she was even stiffer than ever.

She was certainly a mystery, one he wasn't sure he should try to crack. But he'd never be able to resist trying.

As they reached his apartment door, he pulled his keys out of his pocket with a frown as April stepped in front of him and held out a steady hand. She cleared her throat.

"You're taking this protection thing just a little far, don't you think?" he said.

He was immediately contrite. He shouldn't have snapped at her. His irritation had nothing to do with the way she was doing her job.

But she didn't even flinch. "Let me have the key," she said.

"I've got it," he insisted, pushing past her to reach for the lock on his own. "I think I'll be safe enough in my own home."

He threw open the door and flipped the light switch.

The place was trashed.

He'd found no notes this time. Then again, the intentions of the bastard who'd broken in and destroyed his place didn't exactly need to be spelled out any clearer.

April claimed that without a note, there was no way to be certain that the "incident"—as she called it—was related to the threats he'd already received. He begged to differ. She and the police officers could theorize to their hearts' content, but Steve was certain. And he was sure of another thing, too. He'd had enough.

His bristly bodyguard was right. He hated to admit it, but it was past time for him to take this situation seriously. He couldn't wait for these events to escalate any further. It was becoming obvious that the party responsible was taking it seriously, and he couldn't afford for someone to actually get hurt because he was too stubborn to acknowledge the problem.

April glanced his way with a crease digging across her forehead. She said something to the police investigator. It had taken an hour for him to arrive, with two other officers in tow, and he had a feeling it might have taken longer if not for the combination of his reputation and her apparent connections.

Steve had been surprised to hear the investigator call his bodyguard by name and ask after her father. It added another layer to his curiosity about her, but now was not the time for an interrogation…even though the presence of police officers might suggest otherwise.

Doug approached. "I'm so sorry this happened, Mr. Nolan. I still can't believe someone got up here without me noticing and trashed your place. This is completely my—"

"Don't do that to yourself, Doug. It wasn't your fault."

His frown didn't go away. Steve's reassurance wasn't making a dent in the poor guy's guilt. "I'll get the security tape from the manager first thing in the morning and make sure it gets to the cops like I promised," said Doug. "And if I can think of anything else, I'll let Ms. Porter know immediately."

She had asked Doug to outline as much of his shift to the

uniformed officers as he could remember, in as much detail as
he could, indicating that they would record it all and give her
a copy of his statement in the morning. Then she'd supervised
as the investigator brushed Steve's front door and the other
flat surfaces of his office for prints before moving on to do the
same in the kitchen and bedroom.

Steve hadn't had much to do but listen to Doug relating
his statement. He was on nights this week, so he'd started
work at seven that evening and had done a sweep of the
perimeter before the two daytime guards went home. Then
he was the only guard on duty until three in the morning—as
it was, he'd been forced to call in the next guy early when the
police had shown up.

He'd taken a break around ten but ate his snack—a
peanut butter and jelly on rye that his mom had packed—
at the front desk. He'd recalled that there hadn't been any
unaccompanied guests through that evening. It was against
policy to interrogate strangers who *were* accompanied by
residents of the building, so he didn't have a list of those
particular names, but it was a Friday night, so there'd been
plenty of activity.

It was good to know that his neighbors were all having a
good time tonight, Steve thought with a grimace.

He looked around the room, but his gaze always drifted
back to her.

It was obvious that Ms. Porter was the one running the
show here. The investigator seemed competent, but not
invested. After having to explain the threatening letters to
the police once already that day, Steve didn't doubt that if Ms.
Porter hadn't been here now, the cops would have asked him
the same stupid questions all over again. But her no-nonsense
presence had added a degree of efficiency to the procedure
that alleviated a lot of the explosive anger that had consumed
him since he'd walked into his apartment.

A lot of it, but not all of it. There was still enough aggravation there to fuel him for a dozen more hours in the boxing ring.

He fixed his sights on Ms. Porter while he seethed. Maybe she sensed it because she finally nodded and everyone started to pack up. She'd apparently decided they had everything they needed for now. He released a sigh of relief.

The doorman glanced toward her for the twentieth time, too. Doug had been impressed to learn that Steve's guest was actually his bodyguard—he'd decided to confide once the cops showed up—and the guard had been following her movements ever since with something akin to hero worship.

Steve thought he might be feeling the same. Ms. Porter hadn't acted outraged or quit on the spot after he kissed her in the elevator. Instead, she'd stepped up and taken control of this disaster, making the whole thing as hassle-free for him as possible—considering they'd had to call the cops at midnight on a Friday.

She was professional and competent, and he wanted to appreciate her efforts, but this holding pattern was killing him, allowing bitter, unproductive emotions to penetrate the shell of calm he needed to maintain. Someone was bound to find out about this, and if he appeared to be anything other than unconcerned about the whole thing, it would be all over the gossip sites that he'd pitched a fit after "the police had been called to investigate" a "late-night incident" at his home. He could see the headlines twisting it into a domestic dispute, or even worse, actually connecting the dots and linking this to the threatening letters. It never failed to amaze him how easily the facts got warped and corrupted until they barely resembled the truth.

He wanted a pair of boxing gloves and a punching bag, or some other excessively physical activity…and he wanted April Porter. His gaze still hadn't strayed from the figure across the room. He wanted her more than he wanted to breathe. It wouldn't matter if she was wearing Lycra or nothing at all, as long as she was out of that suit.

He gritted his teeth and forced his attention back to Doug. "Hey, why don't you go on home? I think Ms. Porter has everything under control for now, although I'm sure she'll have some more questions for you after she reviews the surveillance video." He clapped the other man on the shoulder. "But you should go home now and get some sleep."

Doug nodded and twisted his hands together as if he wanted to apologize again. "Go," Steve repeated. "There's nothing left to do here tonight."

Doug followed the police officers who were filing out at the same time. The investigator was the last to leave, flipping his notebook closed and putting an arm on Ms. Porter's shoulder as he said good-bye. Steve's gaze narrowed on the point of contact as she reached up and squeezed his hand.

Finally his apartment was empty again, except for Ms. Porter...and the lingering sensation of personal violation as he looked around the room. He supposed that was normal but he refused to give in to it.

"What do you want to do?" she asked, looking around as well. Despite the time, she seemed alert and focused.

He swore. Where was the whiskey? "Catch the bastard who did this?"

It wasn't on the damn sideboard, that was for sure. Nothing was on the sideboard anymore. Whatever *had* been on the sideboard was now in pieces—jagged glass pieces—across the floor, which meant his whiskey was probably soaking into the porous wood grain.

Her mouth tightened. "I meant for right now. Your bedroom seems to have been hit the hardest. The mattress has been slashed, the sheets cut to ribbons. Your clothes are strewn all over the room. Do you want to grab a few things and go to a hotel, or do you have a friend you could call for the night? Maybe the woman you had dinner with earlier this evening? She seemed pretty open to the idea of you staying over." Her tone was distinctly void of emotion once more.

The option was distasteful. He wanted to be at Jennifer's mercy even less now than he had before. "I'm quite sure I'm not up for the kind of payment she would expect in return for a bed to sleep in."

"Oh, I didn't mean that you should…" Wait a minute, was the unflappable Ms. Porter blushing?

He waved it off. "I won't get any sleep tonight no matter where I go. I'll just stay and wade through all this junk to make that list of missing items for the police."

She nodded. "That's fine. Do you want to tell me where to find the other notes then?"

"Now? Shouldn't you be going home to sleep?"

"I can't do my job if I'm at home, and I think it's become more important than ever that I stick close to you."

He snorted. "The security guard in the lobby will be extra vigilant, and your company put extra men outside. Besides, I'm pretty sure the damage has already been done, at least for tonight. Trespassing and vandalism is tiring business. The person responsible is no doubt deeply asleep in his secret lair by now, maybe even wearing a pair of my pajama bottoms."

Her mouth twitched just a little. A tiny smile, and he smiled, too. "It's been a long day for you. Really. Why don't you go home and rest?"

She raised those slim eyebrows and said, "I'll start in the study, then. Didn't you say the notes were in there?"

He grinned. "Well, I've done my gentlemanly duty, but if you really want to spend the night with me, who am I to argue?"

She actually chuckled as she followed him down the hall, but both of them stopped short at the doorway and sighed.

She'd been right that his bedroom had been hit hard, but the office was just as bad. The rest of the apartment had been trashed, too, but it was as if whoever did this had gone into full meltdown mode in these particular rooms.

Steve navigated the books that had been swept off of shelves and the broken glass coating the floor, and carefully stepped behind his desk. It, too, had been swept clean like someone had clotheslined it with his arm. Thankfully, Steve had left his laptop at the office, so it was safe, and there would have been no way to access his confidential digital files from the house even if someone had wanted to try getting around his passwords. But all the desk drawers except for the one he kept locked had been pulled out and upended, and it looked as if all the paperwork had been rifled through.

The locked drawer was scratched up to bejesus, but at least it was still intact. He swept a finger through the greasy fingerprinting dust on the desk with a grimace. The stuff was everywhere, even on the shards of broken glass and some of his paperwork. The police had definitely not wanted to leave any surface untested.

"It looks like whoever did this desperately wanted to get into my files and my desk. When he realized there was nothing here, he apparently went into a rage and tore apart everything else he could get his hands on instead."

"He or *she*," she pressed. "What's in the locked drawer?"

"Not much," he said with a shake of his head. Some reports for surveillance that he'd commissioned on Justin Fielding's family a few months ago after learning that there was a slim chance the man might have survived that car crash after taking off with his father's money. "The anonymous notes are in there, along with some personal stuff, but nothing that a thief would be interested in."

Ms. Porter stepped closer and examined the mess with an objective look of calculation. "This thief, if it was in fact a thief and not just a vandal—"

He snorted. "As if that isn't bad enough?"

"Well, you haven't yet determined if anything is actually missing." That was true. It was also pretty obvious that this was more than a simple robbery. He stifled a shudder. Shit was getting real. He hadn't given any of those notes much consideration one way or another, but this couldn't be ignored. He was able to admit when he'd been wrong, and this time he'd been very wrong.

"The perpetrator is smarter than the average criminal, and it's also likely that this is someone who has a grudge against you personally."

He shook his head. "No. It's not personal. It can't be."

Surprise sharpened her features. "What? You can't still believe...that much has become very obvious."

"Too obvious maybe," he maintained. "Optimus Inc. is negotiating next week for more capital investment, and it's important that both Harrison and I prove that we're solid and dependable, that we have what it takes to bring the company to the next level. It wouldn't take much for a competitor to figure out that our expansion plans could be compromised if the reputation or stability of either one of us was brought into question. It's very possible that all this is being made to *look* personal."

"And you're certain that's the only motivation a person could have to target you?" She paused. "What about your family's past? Could there be any unresolved—"

"No." He didn't want to know what she'd read about his family.

The tabloids had had years to paint the picture of him as a self-indulgent playboy, and most of the time, he was more than happy to go along with it, because it served his purposes to let people underestimate him. But it might be refreshing to one day meet someone who didn't know all about him within moments, and about his family's fatal mistakes.

It was bad enough that the news rags were digging that shit up again because the anniversary of his father's suicide was just a few days away. His mother and sister would be devastated if the media had new fodder for the old scandal.

Grace was almost finished with school and would be moving home to New York in a few months. Mother had finally come out of hiding after letting shame and embarrassment chase her away for years. She'd even started hinting that Steve should marry soon, and from the society women she'd been throwing his way, he didn't have to guess what she hoped to accomplish by such a union. If she could match both of her children with strong, important families, she would have repaired the family reputation in her own way.

They glared at each other until Ms. Porter gave in and nodded. He bent over to pick through a messy pile of papers and tried to determine if anything was actually missing. He thought it was all still there, which wasn't actually good news. It meant that the person responsible hadn't been interested in stealing from him, only messing with him.

He could be wrong about the motivating factor, too. What if it was, in fact, a personal attack? But who the hell could he have outraged so completely?

He looked up and found Ms. Porter gently placing books back on his shelves. She paged through one with a bemused look on her face.

"What?"

She glanced up and showed him the faded brown cover with gold lettering. "*A Treatise of Algebra*?"

"It's rare. 1820s or something. My mother and sister gave it to me for my birthday, the year I graduated high school." The day before the world as they'd all known it had gone up in flames.

The internet made it impossible to leave the past behind.

For the most part, he was resigned to the fact that no matter how successful he became, he would never climb out of the shadow of his father's mistakes, but the idea that Ms. Porter had pored over all that online garbage about his family was surprisingly irritating.

"What kind of guy collects rare *math* books?" she teased, another of those bewitching smiles playing across her lips.

"A *math* geek." He laughed. "But I know what you're thinking."

"You do?" Her slim eyebrow lifted in a perfect arch, and her eyes glittered with humor before she seemed to realize that she'd actually started enjoying talking to him. She looked down and cleared her throat, and he edged a step closer. She was loosening up with him despite herself, and he didn't want her to take it back.

"You're thinking that a guy with my reputation and success already knows everything there is to know about math, and the book is just for show."

She laughed. "Perhaps you should start getting some books on humility then."

He grinned. "I'll keep it in mind."

After a few minutes of an oddly comfortable silence, he recalled her earlier words and said, "So what makes you think the guy who did this is smarter than average?"

"There weren't any prints anywhere, and nobody saw the individual come in or go out." She cocked her head. "Television has made it seem like all violence is committed by criminal masterminds who can only be caught by the most advanced CSI teams in the country, but the reality is that most perps are caught almost before they've even left the scene of the crime."

This was a subject his intrepid bodyguard was obviously very interested in. A simple thing, but her enthusiasm changed her entire face, immediately making her more approachable.

"How does that happen?"

"Mostly, they leave fingerprints. Everyone always thinks they'll never be stupid enough to commit a crime without at least putting on a pair of gloves, but crime is often impulsive and unplanned, and nobody keeps a pair of rubber gloves in their back pocket, just in case. It happens sometimes, but then the perpetrator leaves the scene of the crime and forgets that the trail doesn't end there. They'll drop their name and address at the pawn shop where they're trying to hock stolen merchandise, or they brag about their exploits to their friends in the middle of a crowded bar."

"Next time I think I might break the law, I'm coming to you for planning advice."

She quirked an eyebrow, another one of those fleeting smiles playing about her lips. "Next time?"

He grinned and zipped his lips. She shook her head. "That would definitely involve an additional fee to my regular bodyguard services."

She smiled freely and *didn't* drop her gaze, and his chest swelled in response. *Damn.* Just like he'd thought. He could get used to seeing her smile and listening to her sultry voice. Maybe too used to it, though. And she was most definitely not the right person for him. Prickly and professional, and… and…none of the other reasons were coming to him at the moment.

Wanting to extend the moment despite himself, he asked, "How long have you worked as a bodyguard?"

She paused, and he stilled, waiting to see if she was going to get all stiff on him again, but after a moment she only shrugged. "I guess that means you didn't bother to read my file after your partner hired me?"

"I'm just the numbers guy." He shrugged. "Harrison's a tech genius, and he knows how to bring the investors in. As much as it sometimes pains me to admit it, I trust his judgment."

She winced. "You may not think so once I tell you I've only been doing this for six months."

"How many assignments have you completed?"

"A few. But I guess since I'm admitting things, you should probably know that none of those jobs involved the possibility of corporate sabotage or personal threats."

"Don't worry," he said with a chuckle. "I don't think there's a bodyguard out there more professional or capable, no matter the experience level."

She crossed her arms. "I didn't tell you that because I wanted your approval, but in the interest of fair disclosure. I'll have you know that I've been trained by the best, and as long as I have your cooperation, I *can* help catch this guy for you."

"I have no doubt about it," he assured her, surprising himself because it was true. "But if you haven't been doing this for long, where did you get your FBI contact, and how do you happen to know Investigator Don back there so well?" He was purposely poking just a little deeper into personal territory with every question, hoping to draw out the real April Porter. Every piece of herself that she showed him was more irresistible than the last.

He shouldn't care to know his bodyguard on a personal level. But he did. He wanted it in the worst way. He wanted her to talk to him all through the night and trust him enough to smile without reservation. The feel of her mouth against his in that elevator had been impressed on him, and the taste of her wouldn't be banished until he'd sampled all of her.

"Come on," he said. "You know all there is to know about me. My shit is out there for the whole world's entertainment. Isn't it only fair that I get to know a little something about you?"

She didn't want to share. It was plain on her face.

"If you tell me, I promise to be the perfect body for you

to guard." Given the fact that he had absolutely no intention of opening up himself, the hypocrisy of what he was asking struck him, but not enough that he considered backing off.

But she only snorted and turned away. He swallowed his disappointment, but then she said in a low voice, "I was at the Academy in Quantico, which is how I know a few people in the local FBI office. Don was the police investigator who recommended me for the program. He taught criminology at Berkeley before moving to New York last year. We had a chance to catch up when I came back a few months ago."

"If you went to Berkeley and were in training for the FBI, what the hell are you doing working as a bodyguard now?"

She turned to face him. Her shoulders stiffened. "I didn't flunk out, if that's what you mean."

That's exactly what he'd been thinking at first, but it didn't fit with his impression of her and almost as soon as the assumption entered his mind, he'd already discarded it. "So what happened?"

He could see in her face that she didn't want to talk about it. "Never mind," he said, deciding to lay off. It was surprisingly nice talking to her like this, and he didn't want her to pull away into her impersonal shell again. Normally, he would have kept poking until he'd gotten what he wanted, but she wasn't one of his competitors to be pushed around for profit, and she wasn't one of the selfish social snobs he dealt with to appease his mother. He actually sort of *liked* her.

But to his surprise she said, "I had to withdraw from the program at Quantico because my father's very ill, and he needs me to be here."

"Your mother?"

She pursed her lips. "Died when I was thirteen. Cancer."

He winced. "I'm sorry. But—and don't get me wrong, I'm learning to appreciate having you around—but why are you here with me instead of home with your dad?"

Her eyes glimmered, and he was sorry that he'd brought it up because it obviously made her so sad, she couldn't hold on to her normal cool composure. "He's going through a round of chemo and radiation therapy for the next few days. He's staying at the hospital, and he doesn't want me around."

Steve almost felt guilty for the way he'd been acting. The last thing she needed was to babysit an unappreciative jerk who'd been actively trying to make her life more difficult when all of that was waiting for her at home.

"Don't get me wrong. I like the work, and I could use the extra money to cover some of the bills," she said quickly. Her gaze narrowed as if daring him to pity her. Lucky for her, he wasn't the pitying type.

He pointed to the messy room. "So what kind of evidence should we be looking for to figure out who did this?"

Her shoulders relaxed, and he was glad he'd changed the subject. "Crimes like this are usually domestically connected."

And...she was already back to assuming the attacks were personal. "What are you getting at?"

Her gaze narrowed until he felt as if she might be considering whether or not he'd trashed his own apartment. "I'd like a list of the women you've been seeing recently."

Bitterness stung his throat. "You think I would date someone capable of this kind of violence?"

"Maybe you don't know your women as well as you think you do."

He rounded the desk and closed the distance between them. "I'll let that go because you don't know *me*. But in the future, you might want to refrain from relying on the internet for information about your employers," he said in a tight voice that surprised even him. He prided himself on never letting anyone or anything get to him, but this woman had driven him close to losing his temper more times in just one day than anyone else had in a year.

"I think I have more than enough *personal* evidence to consider that you might be just a little fickle when it comes to women." Her nose tilted stubbornly upward, and her eyes blazed. She was getting him back for that kiss in the elevator. "I still want that list."

"And I'm telling you—for the last time—to leave my personal life out of your investigation." His jaw clenched. He absolutely refused to drag his family through another media hellstorm. His father had put them all through enough of that to last a lifetime.

April didn't know whether to be suspicious or relieved by Nolan's conviction that the attacks against him were not personally motivated.

She agreed that if the anonymous notes were as vague as he'd implied, they could be a strategic ploy by his business competitors to try and discredit him in the eyes of Optimus Inc.'s investors during a crucial phase of the company's development; she'd heard of such things happening. But it also seemed a bit far-fetched. The notes and the vandalism had the earmarks of a temper tantrum, or even a full-blown hissy fit, and in her experience, the old adage was true: the simplest explanation was typically the right one. This felt like an open and shut case of hatred. Pure and simple.

But she supposed it was easy to be philosophical when she wasn't the one who'd been targeted.

She impatiently smoothed away the hair that had fallen across her forehead and tried rolling her shoulders, but the constricting suit jacket wasn't very helpful. She'd been out of the ring for too long if a tiny little sparring match could make her stiffen up so quickly. Maybe she could take her jacket off and—

She shook her head. Taking off that layer of clothing, however decent her shirt was, would be like inviting a more relaxed relationship between them, and she'd already gotten too comfortable too quickly.

"Why don't you take off your jacket?" He was much too observant. "It would probably be more comfortable, especially if we're going to be at this for a while."

He'd shed his and rolled up his sleeves hours ago, and now he tugged at his tie and undid the top button of his shirt, too. She swallowed hard at the glimpse of bronzed skin that suggested he'd recently been somewhere where formal clothing was optional.

"I'm fine." She wasn't normally so stubborn, but something about him made her all too eager to bend, and so she compensated by being more resolute.

"You've been in that suit all buttoned up for most of the last eighteen hours. What do you think will happen if you relax, just a little?"

It *was* warm, and the cheap weave didn't breathe well. The jacket had become more uncomfortable as the long day had gotten even longer. She'd wanted to take it off since she'd been forced to put it back on at the gym, and if the suggestion had come from anyone else she probably wouldn't have thought twice about it.

"I'm perfectly relaxed," she insisted. "Can we just locate the notes and get this place organized?"

He raised an eyebrow. "You're really not cut out to be a bodyguard, are you?"

How could he know after only one day? Even she didn't want to admit it, despite the nervous tic behind her eyes whenever she thought about going from babysitting job to babysitting job for the next twenty years. "Why do you say that?"

"Oh you're capable enough, but you're stubborn as hell,

and you don't have a deferential bone in your entire body." His gaze roamed over her, and he definitely wasn't examining her "bones."

Her cheeks heated. "I didn't realize scraping and fawning over you was a prerequisite for keeping you safe," she snapped.

"Oh it's not," he answered with that playboy grin she hadn't seen in a little while. Her heart sputtered, and she wanted to tell him not to do that again. "But I'm just a spoiled society brat, and if you want me to cooperate, you should probably learn to humor me."

He was teasing her, but she detected a thin thread of sarcasm in his voice. He obviously knew very well who people expected him to be, and instead of bucking the system and showing them all how wrong they were, he played the system, took advantage of it. She had no idea how much of his cheerfully irresponsible personality was real and how much was part of his act, but she also had a feeling that nobody else did either, because Steve Nolan was *always* in character.

"I suppose that bullshit works with your employees, business acquaintances, and maybe even your friends, but I am none of those things," she said tightly. "I'm not here to be your friend or your employee. I accepted this assignment in good faith, and whether you think I'm cut out for it or not, I'll continue to do it until the job is done."

"Yes ma'am," he said with a mock salute. His eyes shone with mirth.

So he thought she was funny, did he?

She shook her head, realizing how quickly she'd risen to the bait and reacted exactly the way he'd expected her to, with righteous indignation. She groaned. Did he get off on antagonizing everyone, or just her?

She was going to have to readjust her expectations. Nolan was turning out to be more complicated than she'd expected.

He played the social playboy character well, but he also had a razor sharp, sardonic wit, and he was brutally observant and surprisingly unpretentious. He didn't fit the stereotypes, and she was embarrassed to have relied on those stereotypes in the first place. In fact, she'd done exactly what she'd expected him to do with her: make generalizations based on appearance, occupation, and background. She'd also broken half the rules that had been drilled into her during training. Never make assumptions. Stay alert. Stay detached.

She worked the buttons and jerked off her jacket, laying it over the back of a leather wing chair that had been slashed all the way down the backrest.

"See, isn't that better?" he said, smug satisfaction dripping from his voice.

She refused to comment. His gaze followed her, but there were no smart-ass remarks about the ice queen finally loosening up.

In the boxing world, she'd gotten that a lot. She had good friends, but there were always overconfident jocks who looked at a woman in gloves with a superior sneer—before making bets on how long it would take to get in her pants. Little had they known that she'd learned from the best in the business. Instead of getting her into bed, she'd let them get her into a ring, and then she'd knocked each one of them on their ass. Sometimes that won their respect and other times...well, she'd learned to deal with that, too.

Only once had she let another boxer get anywhere with her, but that had been different, and that had been...

"You okay? You know you didn't have to take your jacket off if—"

She jerked her head up. "I know," she said. "Let's get back to work. Do you have a safe, or a lock box the perpetrator could have been looking for?"

"I keep a few things in my desk but nothing really

valuable." Nolan pulled a key out of his pocket and wiggled it into the lock on the drawer in his desk. April came around to see. The wood was all scratched up, and the key didn't want to go in at first. The vandal had mucked up the lock trying to jimmy it open. Finally, it slid all the way and clicked.

"What's that?" She pointed to a burgundy folder.

"It's nothing. A surveillance report."

She raised a brow. "You're spying on someone? Don't you think maybe you should have mentioned that when I asked if there was anyone who might have reason to—"

"It's got nothing to do with this."

"Why don't you let the professionals be the judge of that?"

He raked a hand through his hair, obviously frustrated. She sympathized; it had been a long night, but he couldn't keep hobbling her investigation by keeping things from her. She put a hand on his arm. "Nolan, please…"

He jerked his head up, his gaze shuttered and dark with emotion. "I retained the surveillance company because I'd received information suggesting that the man who'd stolen from my father's business was still alive."

"Justin Fielding," she said.

He nodded. "I needed to know for sure."

"What did they find out?"

"Nothing. Go ahead, read it for yourself." He picked up the folder and offered it to her, revealing the handgun that had been in the drawer, beneath the paperwork.

Her heart pounded. "Jesus, don't tell me that's loaded."

"It's not. And it's registered and completely legal," he reassured her.

She still didn't like the idea of him having a gun, but he shoved another handful of papers into her chest and shut the drawer. "The threatening letters."

She reluctantly tucked the surveillance report under her

arm and took the notes gingerly by the corners. "Let me get these into some evidence bags to preserve any fingerprints that might have been left behind."

"There should be something in the kitchen you can use," he said. His arm brushed hers as he slipped between her and the desk toward the door, and both of them froze.

Every one of the earlier feelings that had sent her reeling returned in a rush. His body was still in contact with hers, his arm solid and bulky through his cotton shirtsleeve. He shifted closer and turned his head. His mouth hovered just an inch away. Her breathing hitched.

Then suddenly, her stomach grumbled, interrupting the charged moment.

His eyes crinkled with amusement. "You sat in your car outside the restaurant the entire time I was in there, didn't you?" he asked.

"Of course." She nodded.

He frowned. "I apologize."

"For what?" she asked, surprised.

"For being an insensitive ass," he admitted. "I could have at least sent something out to you."

"It's the job. I'm used to it." Nobody had *ever* wasted a second thought about her diet when she was on a job, not even the little old lady who'd been her last client.

"So when was the last time you ate?"

She'd managed to snag a muffin from Starbucks on the way to his building that morning, but other than that…

"A while," she admitted with a shrug.

He swore and shook his head. "Come with me to the kitchen, and I'll get you something."

Her cheeks heated. "I'm fine. You don't have to—"

He grabbed her hand, pulling her with him. "Don't bother arguing. What good are you going to be to me as a bodyguard if you pass out from malnutrition?"

"I doubt it will come to that." But she was pretty hungry now that she thought about it. In fact, she was getting hungrier by the minute. He still hadn't let go of her hand, so she didn't bother to fight him.

The kitchen was open to a large, informal sitting area with a comfortable-looking sofa and a big-screen television opposite a wall of floor-to-ceiling windows looking out onto the city. Although the more formal main living room at the front of the apartment was nice, it hadn't quite felt like Nolan's style. *This* was exactly where she pictured him spending his personal time. Laid-back, comfortable, and confidently male. It was currently in slightly better shape than the rest of the apartment, but the cushions had still been slashed, and there was a spiderweb crack in the middle of the television, presumably from the stone sculpture lying on the floor in pieces directly beneath it.

He kicked his way to the island in the middle of the kitchen and shuffled through a drawer.

Her throat worked as she stood in place and took it all in. When she'd walked through all the rooms the first time, she'd been focused on making sure whoever had done this wasn't lying in wait for Nolan to return. But now she couldn't help but imagine how she would feel if this was her place.

She was furious on his behalf, but that only reinforced her fear that she'd already gotten much too close to this assignment than was prudent. If she'd been on a case for the FBI, she probably would have been yanked off of it already.

This isn't an FBI assignment. That's not going to be your career now, remember?

She squared her shoulders and took another step forward. A complete set of knives had all been stabbed into the wall over the gas range. Dishes had been taken from the kitchen cupboards and presumably thrown across the room, since they were smashed on the floor all around the fireplace. Not much of it had actually made it *in* the fireplace, so at least she could scratch anyone with good aim from the list of suspects.

Even the refrigerator had been ransacked, a carton of milk dumped out on the floor. Nolan was standing in it. And the contents from a leftover carton of Chinese food was smeared across the countertops. He carefully avoided touching it.

He opened a drawer and found a paper bag and handed it over. She thanked him and folded the notes inside.

He couldn't even hide his disgust as he paused. "There probably isn't anything left in here worth eating," he muttered.

Leaving the surveillance report and bag on a clean square of countertop, April tiptoed through the rubble to the pantry cupboard and peered inside. Whoever had been in Nolan's kitchen hadn't really bothered with it, so the contents were still pretty much intact, although that didn't mean there was much to choose from. She pulled out a lone box of crackers and shook it, then stuck her hand in. They were big and round, and when she popped a whole one into her mouth it stretched her cheeks.

"This will be just fine, thanks." She grinned around a mouthful of crumbs, all semblance of professionalism falling away. It was too late, not to mention she was too hungry and tired, to keep it up any longer.

He came up beside her and looked inside the pantry, too. Then he pulled out a can of sardines and a tiny jar of artichoke hearts in oil.

Hanging from a hook inside the pantry cupboard was a broom. She grabbed it and started to sweep aside the broken china in front of the door.

"Don't do that," he protested, reaching out to stop her. "The insurance company said they'll send someone out in the morning to assess all the damage and start cleaning up."

She felt the urge to comfort him. It had to be hard to be here in the middle of all this destruction. He didn't strike her as the overly sentimental type, but everyone's house should be the one place where they felt safe, the place they kept the things that were special to them. To see everything smashed and broken...

"I just want to clear a spot for a picnic," she said and pointed at the kitchen table, which was covered in half-dried broken eggs that had been smeared around like finger paint. "I'm not sitting there."

With that she plopped down on the floor of the pantry with her box of crackers. He grinned and sat with her, prying the pull-tab lid off the tin of sardines. "Give me one of those," he said. She handed over the crackers with a grin.

He should have looked ridiculous. Cross-legged on the ceramic tile in his suit, minus the jacket, digging into a box of crackers. But as she watched, he bent his leg and draped an arm over his knee. His smile had less of the edge that had crept over him since they'd got here, and her stomach hollowed out with aching desire. He'd only become more appealing with every minute they'd spent together.

He used his fingers to pinch the end of a sardine and put it on his cracker, dripping oil. She looked on in horror as he glanced around for something to wipe his hands with. "Wait!" she cried. "Don't you dare ruin those pants."

He paused and grinned at her. "I have others."

"No you don't," she reminded him, looking back into the pantry. "Not unless you think your devastating smile is enough to keep people from noticing that your clothes have all been slashed to ribbons." She scooted to grab a roll of paper towels from the bottom shelf.

He grinned. "You think my smile is devastating?"

Heat bloomed up to her forehead. "I think you know exactly what you do with your smile, and it's all very calculated."

"Shit. My secret's out." His grin only widened. He tore off

a sheet of paper towel and wiped his fingers. "I guess it's time to drown my sorrows then." He lifted his cracker in a mock toast and popped it into his mouth. Then he went for the jar of artichokes.

She looked on in amazement. "Who even buys this stuff?" she asked with a laugh.

"My parents did all the time. Mostly for the frou-frou cocktail parties they liked to host on Saturday nights." He reached across their makeshift picnic and tapped her scrunched-up nose, smiling when she glared back at him. "But Sunday was the maid's day off, so my sister and I would have to raid the party leftovers because our mother and father went to brunch at the country club."

"They didn't take you with them?"

He shrugged like it didn't matter. "Do *you* know any kids who want to spend their afternoon with the old folks at the country club?" He grimaced as if that was the worst torture a child could be forced to endure.

She took the artichokes from him, making a face at the prospect of dipping her fingers into the oily preservative they'd been packed in. He took the jar back and did it himself, waiting for her to hold out a cracker. "Baby," he teased.

She happily chomped on her cracker and had to admit that artichoke hearts weren't that bad. Weird, but not bad.

Almost like this thing they were doing right now was weird…but not bad.

"Dad took me to the gym every weekend, and I had to meet him there after school during the week," she offered, a little hesitantly. She supposed if he could share, she could, too. "We had a vending machine with chips and stuff, but when the guy came to refill it, he never took the leftover product out, so the old ones just kept getting older and older. I always laugh when I see someone eating hickory sticks, because both my dad and I hated them, and that was the flavor that stayed in the machine the longest."

"Hey, hickory sticks are awesome," he protested, eyes bright with mirth even as he shook his head. "It sounds like heaven."

It hadn't felt like anything special at the time, but when her mother died, her dad had certainly stepped up and attacked the single-parent thing with a vengeance. He'd quit professional boxing and taken a delivery job, but God, he'd been horrible at it. She'd been the one to tell him that he could still do something he loved and be a good dad at the same time, so he'd started training other fighters.

A lot of people might look down their nose at a guy who raised his kid in a boxing club, but at least her dad had been around. April had never gotten away with anything that he didn't find out about.

"Why doesn't your dad want you at the hospital to help him through his treatments?" he asked softly.

She swallowed and glanced away. This was going too far. All this talk of their childhood, asking about her father… She couldn't go there. Not with him.

After a long moment, she simply said, "So, we've got crackers, sardines, and artichoke hearts." She tried to ignore the fact that her throat was tight with unshed tears. "That's got to be at least three food groups right there. What are we still missing?"

Nolan just looked at her, but when she refused to meet his gaze, he finally leaned into the pantry and reached for a box from one of the shelves. She sucked in a breath as his shoulder brushed hers again.

He sat back down and waved a box of chocolate chip cookies in front of her. "Don't forget dessert."

She noted the gourmet label and lifted a brow. "Those are pretty expensive cookies."

"Nothing but the best for my bodyguard." He smiled and

opened the box.

Since coming home to be with her father, there hadn't been a lot of time for the strict workout regimen she'd maintained at Quantico or even while she'd still been boxing. For the first time in her life, she'd had to really watch her calorie intake. "I don't know…"

"Come on, we both need these cookies. Your rockin' bod can handle it, trust me." He looked her up and down with a gleam in his eyes.

She knew she was blushing. She liked the way he looked at her. Unrealistic and probably nothing more than idle flattery, but it made her weak in the knees. Thank goodness she was already sitting.

As they finished their impromptu midnight snack, the discussion stayed pretty easy and lighthearted, but the threads of awareness only strengthened, wrapping around her waist like warm hands and around her throat like silk ribbon. They stayed away from personal subjects and talk about Nolan's stalker. Sitting cross-legged together half inside the shadows of the dark pantry, knees almost touching, she started to wonder if it wouldn't be so bad to explore this attraction that seemed practically unavoidable anyway.

Nolan held out the box of cookies. She took two then watched him devour four in about three seconds flat. "You really like those," she said with a grin when he reached in for more.

"Don't get me started. Last week, there were three of these boxes in the pantry. I have absolutely no willpower when it comes to sweet things." He dropped his gaze to her mouth for about the hundredth time.

Was she just another sweet thing? And when the next one came along, would he have just as little willpower to resist?

She ducked her head and brushed the crumbs from her legs. He got to his feet and held out his hand for her. She looked at it for a second, but it would be ridiculous to refuse. She reached up and let him pull her to her feet before she quickly tugged her hand back.

"I need to apologize," he murmured, still so close that the hair on her arms stood up in reaction to the magnetic field he was throwing off. That's what it felt like anyway, magnets pulling her in.

"For being an unprofessional, inappropriate jerk?" she replied with a grin. She shouldn't talk to him like this. Even though it was long past midnight, they'd just shared a meal, and he looked so tempting her mouth watered just thinking about kissing him again. She had to keep reminding herself that this was a job. And a serial-dating playboy was not her type. Would never be her type.

"Something like that," he agreed, suddenly serious. "I didn't intend to kiss you before."

"Oh." Her heart lurched. She should be glad. This assignment had gone off the rails almost from minute one, and it would be good to clear the air and reset some boundaries—

"But this time I want you to know it's completely intentional." His hand slid up her arm. "There's nothing I want more than to kiss you and keep kissing you until neither of us can breathe, or stand, or think straight."

She already couldn't think straight. The hand on her arm was light, like he wanted to keep her from bolting without actually restraining her. But she was the furthest thing from afraid, at least of him.

His hand tightened on her arm as he leaned closer. His lips moved barely a whisper from hers, she swore she could already feel them tasting her.

"If me kissing you again with absolutely carnal intentions goes against some code of professional bodyguard conduct that you're really determined to maintain, then you should probably—"

"Stop." Her voice croaked, her body protested, but they had to stop. *She* had to stop. No, she wasn't afraid of him, but she *was* afraid of what his touch could do to her sense of self-preservation.

She put her hand up between them against the hard planes of his sculpted chest. He pulled back, his eyes dark pools. *What are you doing? Kiss him!* But nothing good could come from losing herself in Steve Nolan, as much as she ached for that very thing.

Chapter Five

She left like the hounds of hell licked at her heels, slamming the pantry door behind her and leaving him alone in the dark. He bashed his forehead against the door panel and swore.

When he came out, she was already halfway to the apartment door. He caught up to her and held her back. She glanced down at his hand on her arm, and he immediately let her go.

"The guys outside will watch the building overnight. There shouldn't be any danger. You don't need me here." Her voice dripped with ice-cold professionalism as she threw his earlier assurances back at him. "I'll let the doorman know to be extra vigilant until I return in the morning."

And then she was gone.

He wanted to go after her and apologize, but when he almost tripped over his overturned chair and looked at the disaster that used to be his only sanctuary, his home, he let her leave. He was almost as much of a mess as this place and needed to pull himself together.

He was not what anyone would consider a consummate professional on the best of days—life was too short to be so stuffy and serious all the time—but when it came to April Porter, he seemed to lose what little sense he did have. After swearing that he would never give another woman the opportunity to screw him over, he'd gone and shared a family memory with April—whom he'd known for less than twenty-four hours. If the internet was buzzing tomorrow morning about Steve Nolan's fucked-up childhood, it would be exactly what he deserved.

The trouble was, when she'd let down her guard and showed him that brief glimpse of herself, he'd been struck by her humor, her intelligence, her compassion. *That* April Porter had been absolutely irresistible.

He needed a fucking distraction. The apartment walls were closing in. He wasn't going to get any sleep here, didn't want to look at this shit a minute longer...

He grabbed his wallet and keys and headed for the door.

When he exited the parking garage, a car pulled in right behind him almost immediately. He wasn't worried. It had to be April. *April.* She couldn't be Ms. Porter to him anymore; it just didn't feel right. Once you'd had your tongue down someone's throat, it was first names after that, no matter what.

He should have realized the woman wouldn't actually give up and leave. He engaged the vehicle's hands-free system and dialed her cell. "Why the hell are you still here? I thought you were going home."

"Hello Mr. Nolan." Her uber-professional voice was velvety smooth, echoing from the confines of her own vehicle. "Would you like to tell me where you're going at two thirty in the morning?"

What he wouldn't give to have that voice murmuring naughty promises through the line and into his ear. He sighed, focusing on the road. "I needed to get out of there, so I'm going to the office for a while."

"All right." She didn't complain and ask him to turn back around. She hung up without further chitchat.

This time of night, traffic was light, and he was pulling into a space on the street around the corner from the building fifteen minutes later. She'd obviously obtained a parking pass for the building that morning and pulled in behind him as he was getting out of his car. Her hair was down, her jacket was off, and the top two buttons of her shirt had been unbuttoned, like she'd settled in after leaving his apartment, planning on a long night in her car.

She looked deliciously disheveled, but not for long. He watched as she shifted in the driver's seat and looked up into the rearview mirror. She tilted her head back to gather her long hair together and deftly rewound it all back onto her head and secured it in what seemed like one fluid move, before exiting her vehicle and retrieving her suit jacket from the backseat.

Finally she turned to him, eyes flashing. That rock-solid composure of hers must be a bit harder to maintain on almost twenty hours with no sleep. On an average night, even *he* probably would have crashed by now, but the events of the evening had put him on edge, ramping him up even tighter than usual. He needed an outlet, and he needed it bad or his mood was going to go south soon, and hard.

"I didn't intend for you to follow me here. I thought you were going home."

"If you had been able to stay put for more than ten minutes, I might have. But it's a good thing I hadn't left yet because you weren't going to tell the night guards you planned to go out on a midnight excursion, were you? Why didn't you say anything before I left the apartment?" Her words were still crisply formal, but her tone was scorching.

God, she was gorgeous like this. Why would she want to hide such a dominant, fiery personality beneath all that stuffy, businesslike reserve? When did she actually unwind? When was she really, truly herself? With her friends? With a lover?

He wanted to be the one she trusted herself to let go with.

That kind of trust takes time, commitment. That kind of trust was impossible for Steve to give...so how could he expect someone else to grant it to him?

"You were so busy stomping out on me, you didn't ask." That wasn't fair, and he knew it as soon as he said it, but the devil was riding shotgun over his attitude again. Maybe later he'd feel guilty for baiting her, but at this moment he'd do anything to keep April Porter the Amazon from disappearing behind her mask of cool disdain.

She looked like she might bite right through her tongue to keep from snapping at him. If she was holding back out of fear for her job, she needed to know that he would never hold their professional positions against her. "Listen, I want you to feel free to speak your mind. What happened back at the apartment was—"

"Is it your intention to remain in the parking garage for the rest of the night?" She crossed her arms.

He debated the wisdom of having this out with her right now and finally shook his head. He was too keyed up. The last thing he needed was to lose control and make another move on her and have the papers painting him as a dirty, sex-crazed deviant in the morning. She'd made her feelings clear. He had to get control of himself.

"Let's go," he said.

After hours, all employees used a key card to access the building, which included the elevators. This time they rode up in complete silence, perched at opposite ends of the car. Her jaw was clenched tightly. He'd noticed earlier that her stiffness in the elevator wasn't only because of his presence. When the door slid open and they stepped out, she seemed to take a deep breath, as if she'd been trying not to breathe at all while locked up in the box.

He unlocked his office door, but let her slip in ahead of him. She motioned for him to stay put while she entered and looked around. Impatient, he did what she asked and waited.

Finally, she turned to him and nodded. "All clear. Thank you," she said.

He understood that she was thanking him for letting her do her job and felt a rush of guilt. She veered wide as she walked past him, heading for the door. "I'll wait outside until you're ready to leave."

He spun around. "Why don't you stay?"

She stopped with her hand on the door and shook her head. "You were right. I don't need to sit on top of you to do my job."

He reached for her hand. She jerked her head up, eyes wide. "Stay," he repeated. "I could use the company."

She hesitated.

A rueful smile pulled at his lips. "I promise I won't try to kiss you again...tonight." He couldn't promise more than that.

He made his way behind his desk and sat down, leaving the decision to her. He fired up his laptop and felt a zing of hope when she turned away from the door and went to the big windows of his office instead.

With a last look at her incredible silhouette against the backdrop of New York at night, he knew he had to focus on the economic projection report Harrison needed for Monday, or else he *would* end up kissing her again.

When he blinked and glanced away from the computer screen hours later, he realized it was five a.m., and April wasn't standing by the window anymore. He stood abruptly and started for the door before noticing that at some point she had lain down on the couch across the room.

She was fast asleep.

He stopped as close to her as he dared without waking her. Her arms curled around herself and her knees were drawn up. Her chin tucked in, as if she felt the need to protect herself even in sleep. But her features had softened, her forehead smoothed out, and her lips parted slightly. She looked so young, so soft, like a fairy princess. The fact that she was really an Amazonian *warrior* princess made him smile.

Protection was more than just an occupation for April Porter. This was a woman who had given up her bright future to care for her dying parent, and then taken a crappy job watching out for an ungrateful jerk like him because she needed money to pay the medical bills.

They might seem like complete opposites, but he understood her. On a dark and stormy night ten years ago, the first anniversary of his father's death, he'd found his mother crying in her room, the same as every night, and promised her that one day he'd be able to fix it all. He'd promised she wouldn't have to lock herself in the house alone anymore, that Grace would be able to come home from school and not be the subject of gossip, and they wouldn't have to be embarrassed to carry the name Nolan. He was going to fix it so she could hold her head high.

It might not have looked like he'd done anything about it in the years since, as if he didn't have a care in the world. But that was because he hadn't wanted anyone to know how much he wanted it. Showing desperation or need was the kiss of death in the kind of circles over which the Nolan family used to reign.

And now here he was on the cusp of financial success the likes of which his father could never have accomplished. He could walk into any country club in the city, and he could have any number of women with powerful social connections. His mother had finally stopped crying.

He looked down at the tough, defensive woman who threw a punch like a pro and stood up to him like an equal. The beauty sleeping on his couch who wouldn't last a minute in that world.

Chapter Six

April opened her eyes with a gasp. It took her a moment to remember where she was.

Nolan's office. Nolan's couch.

She was alone. Nolan was gone.

She jumped up, tripping over the blanket she didn't remember being there when she'd lain down.

She swore a blue streak and was halfway across the room when the door to the private bathroom opened, and there he was, wearing nothing but a big white towel, steam still rising around him and moisture clinging to his decidedly distracting body.

"I didn't ditch you," he said with a grin, leaning against the doorjamb.

She swallowed and nodded, aware she was staring but unable to look away. "Uh, yes. Good. Thanks."

He watched her, obviously enjoying her reaction. Self-conscious, she raked a hand through her hair and pushed it off her shoulders. "Shouldn't you maybe…" She pointed to the towel. The only thing keeping it clinging to his hips was a little tuck of the corner.

His grin widened, and he put his hands on his hips. She bit her lip. "Just put *something* on, please," she begged. "I can't talk to you like that."

He chuckled and her cheeks burned. "I'll be back out in a minute, then you're welcome to use the shower in here if you want to freshen up."

She closed her eyes as soon as the door closed again, but that only sharpened the picture in her mind.

What time was it? The last thing she remembered before falling asleep was checking her voicemail. Her phone was probably somewhere in the couch cushions now. She went back and found it sitting on the side table. She couldn't recall having put it there herself, but it was possible. She knew that she hadn't gotten herself a blanket, though. Which meant Nolan had covered her up while she slept. Her cheeks heated again, but she shook it off and called her dad.

"April?"

Her heart lurched. He sounded weak and tired. "Dad, are you okay?"

He coughed. "I'm fine. Where are you?"

She needed to go to him. She'd call the office after she got off the phone and arrange for someone else to relieve her with Nolan for a few hours. She blinked back tears and forced a normal tone into her voice. "On a job. I'm so sorry I didn't get back to check on you last night, I—"

"No. I told you not to come, and I meant it. It's just me sitting in a chair with a needle in my arm, getting crankier by the minute. I don't need you for that. Besides, Grady's gonna come in a little while and bring me coffee. The stuff here tastes like motor oil." Grady was her dad's old coach and best friend, who'd taken over the gym when he got too sick to run it himself.

She chuckled, even though all she wanted to do was cry.

"Dad, I want to be there. I'll just sit with you and—"

"I don't want you," he snapped.

She hissed. "But you want Grady?" she said, hurt.

After a long moment, he sighed over the line. "I'll call if I need something."

He hung up.

She stared down at the phone, feeling angry and powerless. Her father had never spoken to her like that before. Since her mother died, it had been the two of them against the world, but then he'd gotten sick and had been withdrawing from her, especially ever since she'd said she was coming home. She had thought it would get better with her there, but if anything, things between them were worse.

Someone cleared their throat behind her. She spun around to find Nolan frowning at her. "Is everything all right?" he asked.

She swiped the tears from her eyes and looked away. "Yeah, it's fine."

"Is it your father? Do you need to go to him?"

"My father is fine," she said sharply, regretting everything she'd ever mentioned about her personal life. She didn't need his pity. She squared her shoulders and looked him up and down. "Is that what you're going to wear the rest of the day?"

He glanced down at his gym shorts and tank top. "Is that your way of saying this would be inappropriate for a Saturday afternoon out on the town?"

She hoped he couldn't see her blush. Who wouldn't enjoy that view? But he was even more distracting than usual like this. He flexed his pecs and watched for her reaction. Yep, he knew she was blushing.

"Apparently this is all I've got left right now. As much as I hate the idea, I'm going to have to go shopping. I suppose you'll want to come?"

She blamed her smile on having just awakened and quickly

renewed her determination to keep Nolan at a distance. As a woman who'd spent a lot of time around hormone-driven, muscle-bound men in gym shorts and boxing gloves for most of her life, she was used to being pursued. But for most of those men it had been all about the challenge, and she'd seen right through it. Jeremy hadn't been a part of that world; he'd been different, and she'd fallen for it. He had tricked her into believing he was interested in *her*, and in the end, that's why he'd been worse than the others.

She refused to be the means by which another guy stroked his own ego.

"I suppose I have no choice but to go with you. We can't set you loose upon an unsuspecting populace looking like that, or we'll have a female riot on our hands. I'm not that good at my job." She started for the bathroom. "I'll be out in ten minutes."

When she came out exactly ten minutes later, she felt a little better but wished she had something to wear besides her suit. She hadn't planned on providing twenty-four hour protection and would have to call for a replacement at some point, if only to go home and grab a change of clothes.

"There's no need for us to take separate cars," he said when they entered the parking garage, which was still pretty empty on this Saturday morning.

She nodded. "Fine. I'll drive." She started to get in her car but turned back around at the sound of his locks clicking open and saw Nolan sliding into the driver's seat of his own vehicle.

"Get in," he called.

He was already starting the engine. She gritted her teeth and opened the passenger side door. "Why do you get to drive?"

"I'm the boss," he said, revving the engine.

"I beg to differ," she snapped. "You might be the client,

but you are *not* my boss."

"Then, because my car is nicer."

She couldn't argue with that. She drove a perfectly respectable black Honda that was less than three years old, but it was a clunker next to his Mercedes. And as she sat down, the buttery leather interior and tinted windows made her feel like she'd just slipped into his private den, complete with soft classical music.

"Do you listen to this a lot?" she asked, curious.

"The music?" He looked at her. "Do you want me to change it?"

"No, it's fine. I guess I just pictured you as more of a hard rock kind of guy."

"Why do you say that?"

She shrugged. "Those kinds of heavy, energetic beats seem to match your active…personality."

He raised a brow at her delicate choice of words as he glanced into the rearview mirror and reversed out of his parking spot. "What do you like to listen to?"

"Nothing in particular." They exited the parking lot, and the morning sun bounced off the chrome detail around his windshield. She tipped her head back to soak it in.

"'Fess up. You're a closet country music fan, aren't you?"

Her mouth fell open. "How did you know?"

"Because country music is sincere and unapologetic, just like you."

She blushed and looked down at her lap. "This is a beautiful car," she said, letting her fingers trace the stitching in the seat beside her thigh. "I thought you and Mr. Harrison were looking for more investment money to expand your company?"

He chuckled. "The kind of money we need at this point in the game isn't going to happen just because I save a couple bucks driving a Toyota instead of a Mercedes. In fact, it's more important than ever that it appear as if the money is rolling in. Everybody wants to jump on board the rocket ship, not the sinking ship."

Forty-five minutes later, having thankfully stopped for coffee and muffins, they walked through the front door of an exclusive men's shop. It was very different from women's clothing stores—at least the ones she shopped at—she couldn't really say she was an expert on shopping for any sex.

It was big and open, with dark wood floors that had been covered with different sized high-contrasting geometric rugs. The mannequins were all faceless chrome figures that reminded her of an old sci-fi movie she'd seen on late-night television a while ago, and the clothing racks were almost bare—which she supposed was designed to give the illusion of exclusivity.

A salesclerk with a sleek silver tag identifying him as Jerry greeted them as they entered. He reached out eagerly to shake Nolan's hand and looked April up and down curiously, as if he wasn't sure they were really together, or if two strangers had just happened to walk into his shop at the same time.

Nolan explained that there'd been a "mishap" and his closet had suffered. "I've got to get a few things to last the rest of the week. What have you got that I can take home today?"

Jerry frowned. He didn't like the idea of selling something "off the rack."

April stood back and let Nolan and Jerry have their fun. She wandered a little and found herself looking down at a table of cashmere sweaters. She ran her hand over a black one and looked up at Nolan. It would look great on him.

She found him watching her and jerked her hand back. She was so *not* picking out clothes for Steve Nolan.

He finally made his way to the changing room. April waited in a very comfortable leather club chair with her coffee and tried not to think about the fact that he was stripping down to his skin not ten feet away from her.

Thankfully, he didn't come out and model for her, and after another ten minutes, Jerry was packing up four bags worth of clothing, and Nolan was wearing a pair of dark blue jeans with a white T-shirt beneath the same black cashmere sweater she'd been eyeballing earlier. She hadn't even seen him go pick it up.

"How do I look?" He held out his arms and grinned.

So good she ached just looking at him…and he had to know it. But more than the way he looked, it was that easy smile and overwhelming confidence that got to her. "Fine," she said tightly, glancing away quickly. "Are you ready to go, then?"

He chuckled knowingly and tossed the garment bag over his shoulder. "Thanks for your help, Jerry."

The salesman walked them to the door and said good-bye with a wide smile. Why not? He'd probably just made his sales quota for the day.

April refocused on her job as they left the store. She watched the street, but it was a busy Saturday morning, and the sidewalks were crowded. She scanned faces, but noticed nothing out of the ordinary. Just young, trendy-looking shoppers out on a Saturday morning. So then why did her defenses suddenly go up with an electrical zap down her spine? She tensed, her senses sharp. She had the strongest sensation that she'd seen something important, but that her brain hadn't yet identified it.

She stopped walking and put a hand on Nolan's arm.

"What is it?" he asked.

Her lips pressed together. "I don't know, but…something." She kept her eyes peeled. "I need to get you off the street."

He didn't argue or question her, simply took her hand and pulled her into the next shop. April barely noticed that it was a women's clothing store. She stayed to the side of the door behind a rack and looked out the window, watching to see who might have stopped when they ducked inside, or might be staring in after them. But of the passersby, none seemed to show any outward interest.

Just as she was about to chalk up her reaction to lack of sleep and nerves, a man stepped in front of the store window. Fairly young, no older than she was anyway. He wore dark glasses, but it was a sunny morning, so that shouldn't have bothered her. And yet, something about him set off warning bells. He peered through the glass, but he wasn't interested in the window display. His gaze sharpened, and he seemed to tense. She knew he was looking at Nolan.

She stepped out from behind the rack, catching the stranger's attention. He glanced up and looked right at her for a split second before abruptly turning his head. He started walking. She pushed open the door to follow at the same time a woman and a teenaged girl stepped up to the entrance. They danced around each other in the bottleneck doorway, and by the time April managed to squeeze by them and get outside, there was no sign of the suspicious man.

Nolan had followed her outside. "What was that about?" he asked.

She took his arm and pulled him back inside the store. "There was a man standing outside the shop window, looking in. Have you seen him before?"

He frowned. "I didn't see him now. What did he look like?"

She glanced back through the window, recreating the image of the figure who'd been there just a moment ago in her head. "Tall, slender, but wiry, and...scrappy."

"How can you tell that someone is 'scrappy' by looking at him?" he asked.

"I've been around the type my whole life. The stiffness in his shoulders, and his nose was crooked, like it'd been broken a couple of times, and there was a focused look in his eyes. He wasn't looking at the dresses, I know that much." She shrugged, feeling suddenly uncertain. After all, until this moment she would have bet money that they were dealing with a woman.

Could she be imposing qualities on perfect strangers simply because she was trained to look for trouble? It wasn't completely unheard of in her profession.

"He also had light brown hair, on the long side like he's a couple weeks overdue for a haircut but not purposely going for a shaggy look. I'm pretty sure he had brown eyes, and he was wearing slim-fitted blue jeans and a sweater beneath an overcoat that seemed much too heavy for June." She outlined what she could remember out loud, more for herself than for him, to commit the image to memory so she could recall the information later if it became necessary to do so.

"That's a decent description, but there's got to be a billion tall, brown-haired guys in the city."

"Staring through a women's clothing store window?"

"I didn't say he wasn't a creeper, but looking at women's clothes doesn't necessarily make him *my* creeper."

Nolan was right. The guy could have been looking at something for his girlfriend and gotten embarrassed when he realized she'd noticed him.

She still felt like there was more to it than that, but she couldn't go after the guy now. He was probably already long gone anyway, and her job was to stick with Nolan. Besides, as suspicious as he'd seemed, something about this guy being Nolan's stalker didn't feel right.

"Are you absolutely certain you haven't seen a woman?" she asked.

He blew out an impatient breath. "This again? What woman in particular should I have noticed?"

"Long nose, long black hair. I'm almost positive I saw her

last night outside the restaurant." She paused as something came back to her. That hadn't been the only time. "She was also in your office building yesterday afternoon. I remember seeing her in the elevator."

"There are about as many black-haired women in New York as there are brown-haired men, but to be fair, I don't think I know anybody by that description," he said, surprisingly calm.

She lowered her voice and dared a little more. "Are you sure you haven't ended any relationships recently? With anyone at all?"

For the first time, he didn't rail at her for bringing up the crazy old girlfriend theory, but the look in his face was pinched. "Contrary to what the rags might say, I don't make a habit of being careless—at least not anymore. The women I date understand that my business comes first and that I'm not interested in putting the time and energy into a long-term relationship. They're just as career-oriented and only want to relieve some of the stress that comes with a high-powered job, have some fun."

Her lips compressed, and she nodded. "It sounds very… convenient for everyone."

"You probably wouldn't understand."

She crossed her arms. "You're right, I'm no high-powered executive. Just a lowly bodyguard who couldn't possibly relate to her betters."

His forehead creased in a frown and he shook his head. "That's not what I meant."

"I know what you meant. Let's just get back to the point." She glanced over at the store window. "If you still believe that none of the women you've been with could have misunderstood your intentions, then who am I to—"

His posture tightened suddenly.

"What is it?" she asked.

He opened his mouth, then shook his head. "Probably nothing."

April wanted to hit him. He saw the look on her face and said, "Okay, okay. There was an incident with a woman last year in Antigua. A journalist. She fixated on me and used her reporter credentials to follow me to a business convention there. She tried sneaking into my hotel room one night, and I had to call security to have her removed."

"Did you sleep with her?"

"We had dinner before I found out she was a reporter, and there may have been a couple of after-dinner drinks involved," he admitted with a grimace. "Trust me, if I'd known what she was beforehand, I wouldn't have gone near her with a ten-foot pole."

"Why didn't you say anything about this earlier?"

"There wasn't much more to it than that, and it was over a year ago. Besides, there's been no sign of her since then, and she was definitely a blonde."

April filed the information away. "Women change their hair color all the time. I'm going to look into it," she warned him. "I want to find out where this journalist is now, and what she's been up to."

His jaw clenched, but he still hadn't told her again to back off. They were making progress.

Finally, he nodded. "All right. Her name was Victoria or Veronica something. Ash, I think. Veronica Ash. She was with the *Times*, but I think after the incident at the hotel…I don't know if the paper dropped her or she just went somewhere else."

Of course he barely remembered the woman's name. Just like he would be unlikely to remember hers a year from now if she let herself be stupid enough to fall for his charm. April took out her phone and recorded the information.

"What about the guy at the window?" he asked.

"I'm going to find them both, and then we'll see," she said. Adrenaline surged. At least she had something to go on. She smiled.

"Excuse me, miss? Sir? Is there anything that I can show you today?"

April had almost forgotten where they were. She turned to face a stunning salesclerk who happened to be modelling the exact outfit that was being displayed on the mannequin beside her—and it looked better on the clerk, too. "No," she said just as Nolan said, "Yes, we need a dress."

She spun around to face him. "What?"

"Give us a minute," he said to the salesclerk, as if she would just wait at attention until he decided he was ready for her…which she probably would. From the sparkle in her eyes, she'd either recognized him or she was plotting ways to slip him her number.

Maybe both.

He gave April one of those appraising looks that was both appreciative and calculating at the same time. "I have an event to go to this evening. I assume we'll still be stuck with one another, so you'll have to come with me."

That wasn't remotely how she'd always imagined being asked on a date, but of course, he hadn't been talking about a date.

"Since you're trying to dress me again, I assume it's not a tractor pull. What kind of event are we talking about?"

He paused, and his features tightened almost imperceptibly. "It's a charity event that my mother has organized to raise money for the Suicide Hotline…in memory of my father."

His expression told her all that she needed to know about how much he wasn't looking forward to it. "If this thing is tonight, haven't you already asked someone to be your date?"

He shook his head. "There wasn't anyone I wanted to go with before now."

"And you think taking your bodyguard will be romantic?"

"I think taking my bodyguard will kill two birds with one stone. I won't have to explain to a date why there's a shadow accompanying us, and I won't have to deal with my mother throwing eligible women at me all night either."

That's right, his mother had been playing matchmaker. "What makes you think I don't already have something appropriate?" Granted, she had no idea where any of her dresses were. After moving back home, all the things she hadn't thought she would need for a while had gone into storage to save space in her father's tiny house in Brooklyn.

He smiled and turned to the salesclerk, who had unobtrusively, but curiously, been watching. "Find us something in black." The woman smiled and moved away to do just that.

"I don't need a dress," April insisted. "I assume there will be security at this event. I can wear a suit and blend in with the rest of the standard detail."

He took her hand and leaned in close enough to whisper in her ear. "If something happens, you'll beat yourself up if you're not right there, right by my side." His voice caressed her with the same softness and promise as his fingers did her wrist.

She cleared her throat. "Fine, I'll go. But this isn't a date, so I don't need a dress."

"Maybe not, but it needs to look like a date," he insisted. "Besides, you can't dance if you don't wear a dress."

"Dresses and dancing aren't part of my job description," she said stubbornly.

"You know, just to make it feel real, I should have asked you properly." He lifted her fingers to his mouth. Her breath caught when he stopped less than an inch from touching her and looked into her eyes. Her heart raced. "I'm a little rusty at this," he murmured. "I haven't asked a woman out on a date in a long time."

She snorted. "You can't expect me to believe that."

"Sadly, it's true. I'm not saying I don't get dates, but…" *He doesn't have to ask.*

"This isn't necessary." She started to pull back again, but he twined his fingers with hers and laid his warm, supple mouth on her knuckles. She froze, holding her breath and her body, and…everything.

"April Porter—" Her name came from his lips like velvet, like he savored the feel and taste of it. "Would you honor me with your company this evening?"

She opened her mouth, but before she could answer, he turned her hand over and pressed a kiss in the sensitive middle of her open palm. She groaned silently and pulled back, closing her hand into a tight fist as if she could keep the feel of him right there.

She cleared her throat. "I already said I would go."

"Because it's your job, or because you want to dance with me so badly?" His mouth twitched with devilment. She wondered if he'd ever been sincere for longer than a heartbeat.

She couldn't help but smile back. "I'll go because you asked so elegantly."

The pretty clerk came back then, and April agreed to try on a few dresses. "But *if* I get something, I'll be paying for it myself," she said to Nolan sternly.

He shrugged and followed her to the back of the store. Here, too, there were comfortable chairs for those stuck waiting, and Nolan crashed into one with the look of a person who'd just realized he hadn't slept in over twenty-four hours.

She entered the changing room just as he laid his head back and closed his eyes. She tried on three of the black dresses without feeling much excitement about any of them one way or the other, even though the salesclerk had done a good job estimating her size. The last dress wasn't actually black. It was a deep cobalt blue. It slid over her curves like it was made for her, and it brought out the color of her eyes.

She took it off and pulled on her suit pants and shirt before folding the garment over her arm. She opened the door. The saleswoman threw a bemused glance at the big man sleeping in the chair. "Out like a light," she whispered. "I've had a few husbands doze off after an hour or so waiting for their wives to make a decision, but never in less than five minutes."

"It's been a long few days," April explained. She handed over the dress. "I'll take this one."

"I was hoping you would say that," she said with a satisfied smile. "I know it isn't black, but I took a chance because the cut is fantastic." As the woman went up front to wrap it, April allowed herself to look at Nolan. The kink in his hair beckoned, and she was reaching out to run her fingers through it when she realized what she was doing and stopped herself.

"Not sleeping," he said. She gasped and stepped back. He hadn't moved a muscle, but his eyes had opened and his stare was focused and intent. Her stomach fluttered with anticipation, and she wished she had put her suit jacket back on again. "Just resting my eyes."

She braced herself, waiting for him to say something inappropriate or teasing, but he didn't. Finally, she looked away first. "I'll just finish getting dressed and then we can leave."

He nodded, still not moving. Out of the corner of her eye, she could see that he was still watching her.

Suddenly, the sound of a cell phone ringing filled the space between them. She instinctively patted her pocket, but it wasn't hers. Nolan pulled his phone out and glanced at the display before answering it. "Hi," he said with a devastating smile that made April want to sink into the floor. "When did you get back from France?"

She turned and went back into the changing room to put on her jacket. His voice lowered to a soft, intimate murmur that she wished she couldn't hear…but she did.

She couldn't help but listen to the one-sided bits and pieces of a conversation that sounded very much like a man reassuring his lover that everything was all right. "Meredith, it's nothing. Of course I'm being careful…yes…no…I promise…soon then."

It was impossible to miss the affection he had for the person on the other end of the line…*Meredith*. But last night he'd been with Jennifer, and then he'd kissed *her*.

Part of her had begun to think that maybe the news rags had been exaggerating when they painted Nolan as a womanizing playboy, but obviously she'd been wrong. Falling into bed with him and becoming just another of the women he kept dangling around would be an even worse mistake than falling for Jeremy had been. At least with Jeremy, there'd been no way for her to know in advance the games he was playing with her. But now, all the signs and warnings were there, and if she ended up another notch on Steve Nolan's belt, it would be all her own fault.

She waited until she was sure he'd hung up the phone before she came back out of the changing room.

"I, ah, don't think I need a dress after all," she said, focused on buttoning her jacket. "If you still require protection this evening, my original plan to stand watch from the sidelines will be more than adequate."

He stopped her when she tried to breeze past him, slipping his hand to the back of her neck so she had to look up at him. She was mortified to realize that even now she wanted to lean into his touch, lift her mouth for his kiss.

"Meredith is just a friend. A good friend, but nothing more."

She set her jaw. "It doesn't matter. This is just business,

remember?"

"Buy the dress, April."

He made her first name sound like an order. She set her jaw, but she bought the dress to keep from making a scene in front of the salesclerk. When they left the store, both of them carrying garment bags this time, April scoured the area for the man she'd spotted earlier.

"Do you see anything?" Nolan asked as they got to the car. He stood back and let her do a walk-around.

Her throat tightened as she got to the rear passenger side of the vehicle. "Besides your slashed tire, you mean?"

Chapter Seven

The replacement bodyguard hung up the phone. "Sir, Ms. Porter has had your car towed to the address of the garage you gave her, and the insurance company will be dropping off a rental for your use shortly."

A half-full glass of scotch in his hand, he turned away from the window and walked back to his desk without acknowledging the guy.

After examining Steve's car for further damage, April had immediately called both the police and her agency. Ten minutes later, a car had pulled up, and John the replacement bodyguard here had brought him back to his apartment while she stayed behind to deal with the cops.

He circled his glass on the oak, leaving behind a ring of moisture. "If you have to stick around, I'd prefer it if you waited outside." He was wound up, feeling provoked, powerless, and hostile, and he shouldn't take it out on this guy.

If April had been there, she would have arched those delicate eyebrows that hid so much stubbornness and stayed right where she was anyway, but this guy only shrugged and nodded. "If you need anything, that's where I'll be."

He didn't resent April's presence as his bodyguard anymore. In fact, he trusted her—up to a point, at least. He couldn't trust her with his personal life, but he trusted her dedication to her job. She wanted to find out who was stalking him. To that end, she'd been working nonstop since the moment she walked into his office yesterday morning, and she was still working.

If only he didn't want her so badly, he might be able to appreciate her efforts and get back to work himself, but he hadn't been able to focus.

It's just because she's an anomaly. A beautiful, stubborn, intriguing anomaly.

Getting her into a dress and bringing her to an event like the gala tonight among all the people he knew would help him see that she was no different than any other woman. With the attention on her as his date, once the cameras flashed and the champagne flowed, she would seek to extend her fifteen minutes of fame, just like they all did, and that would help him get her out of his system.

He turned his attention to the destruction of his apartment. The cleaners had been in and done a good job clearing the majority of the mess, but there was still a lot to go through.

He'd been able to confirm that there really wasn't anything missing except for a box of photos from his bedroom and a gold ring that had been his father's. Grace had asked him for photos a few weeks ago to use at the memorial service tonight, so he couldn't be sure if those had actually been stolen or if she'd simply come to get them and forgot to mention it. He'd wanted no part of anything to do with their father, so he may have blocked out the day she stopped by. He made a mental note to call home and ask. If nothing else, his mother and Grace deserved to know what was going on. He doubted that any of this would spill over onto them, but he should warn them to be careful nevertheless.

After two hours with nothing to do but assess his every acquaintance as a possible suspect, he was climbing the walls. He decided to go to the club and had just grabbed his bag when there was a knock at the door.

He knew it was April from the three quick, sharp raps against the wood-paneled surface. Precise. Decisive. Unflinching.

He opened the door. She'd changed into tight jeans and a tailored leather jacket that looked much more her style than yesterday's ugly suit. In fact, he couldn't take his eyes off her legs and ass as she pushed past him into his foyer.

"Why is John out here?" she asked, frowning fiercely.

"Because I didn't want him inside."

"He can't assist you from the other side of a locked door."

"Then it's a good thing I didn't need his assistance," he snapped. His temper had reached the boiling point. "You're here now anyway, so it makes no difference to anyone what he can or can't do."

"I know how the stalker got past security and up to your apartment last night."

That wasn't what he'd been expecting. "Did he slip in with another resident?"

She shook her head, the exhilaration of her breakthrough shining from her eyes. Some of his irritation bled away just watching her. "He took the stairs. I checked. There are no cameras in the stairwell, and the emergency door on the main level exits off the side of the building into the alley."

He frowned. "Sure, but the door automatically locks when closed, and only opens from the inside."

"Yes, but it wouldn't take much to come into the building some other time of day and slip a piece of paper into the mechanism to keep it from latching. The security guards wouldn't necessarily have noticed it because the door would still close, and there'd be no way to tell that the lock wasn't engaged unless they physically checked. I'm betting your stalker took a gamble that the security guards weren't that industrious."

"That explains the how then, but still not the why or the who."

Her face was flushed with animation. He found himself transfixed, fascinated by her exhilaration. She grinned. "But I think I know the who, as well."

He stopped. "Really?"

She nodded. "The same guy from the store this morning."

"How do you know that?"

"Because I just talked to Doug downstairs. He showed me the building's surveillance tapes. From seven thirty to eight thirty yesterday morning, when many of the building's residents are leaving to go to work for the day, the cameras picked up a man standing just outside the front doors, watching people leave as if he was waiting for someone in particular. The picture's a little grainy, but it's the same guy, I'm sure of it."

"And you think he was waiting for me?" Steve had left for the gym at around six that morning and had gone straight to the office afterward, so he would have missed the guy. "If he was loitering there for so long, why didn't the security guard notice? They should have gone out and got him moving along, or at least asked him what he was doing there."

"He stood just out of view of the front doors but probably didn't realize he was on camera. Besides, your morning guard is apparently a really friendly guy. He likes to stand out from behind the security desk to say hello to all the residents, so he wasn't watching the screens and obviously didn't notice."

Yeah, Billy loved to chat. He knew who to discuss last night's hockey game with and who'd be up for a rousing discussion about politics. He even talked to Mrs. Tobin from the tenth floor about her knitting projects. "Okay, but who is he?"

She frowned. "That we don't know yet. But I'm going to send the surveillance image to my friend at the FBI, and I've already stopped by the station to finalize the police reports from last night's incident and this morning's slashed tire. They have a copy of the tapes now, too, and I gave them a description of the man I saw. I also gave them the other notes. They'll see what they can come up with and be in touch."

She was brimming with accomplishment and optimism, but he wasn't about to hold his breath that the police or FBI would have anything to report. They were still trying to figure out if the man who'd embezzled millions of his family's money was actually dead or alive. No, if anyone might solve this thing, it was going to be April Porter. Surprisingly, he believed in her more than he'd believed in anything else since his father's suicide.

"I assume we can't do anything about it for the time being?"

She shook her head. "Not until I get a hit on this guy's identity, but I'm hopeful that we'll have something before the end of the day."

He should be grateful, but he found himself unreasonably hoping that didn't happen, at least not until after the charity gala. He had a feeling April was going to disappear from his life as soon as her assignment was over, and he realized he wanted at least one opportunity to dance with her before it happened. "Then I'm going to the club." He hefted his pack over his shoulder. "Are you coming?"

She looked taken aback, as if she hadn't noticed the gym bag in the excitement of her breakthrough. "Oh. Yes, sure."

They left the apartment, but Nolan bypassed the elevators.

Her gaze narrowed. "Why are we taking the stairs?"

He shrugged. "It's good exercise, right?"

Since she'd avoided the elevator on the way up to this floor, she knew exactly how good the exercise was, but she wasn't about to tell him that.

He pushed open the door and started down.

"Whoever broke into your building came up the stairs," she reminded him.

"Well, we've got to catch this guy sometime, right?" He pushed through the heavy fire door.

"If you insist on this course, then at least let me go first to make sure the way is clear."

"Can you honestly say that you think someone's lying in wait for me on the tenth floor landing?" He pointed to the emptiness ahead of them, his voice bouncing off the concrete walls.

"Did *you* think your place was going to get trashed?" she asked, even though she was pretty sure everything was fine. After all, she'd been up those stairs not ten minutes ago and encountered absolutely nobody. "Didn't you promise to be the perfect body for me to guard just last night?"

He laughed and swept his arm out with a flourish. "You're right, I did. Please protect me from the stairwell dust bunnies."

She stepped ahead of him. He may still be giving her grief, but some of his indignation had faded at least.

Four floors later, with eleven still to go, she broke down and asked, "What's the real reason you didn't want to take the elevator?"

"Getting tired?" He grinned. They descended side by side. She could have insisted he stay behind her, but she didn't press her luck. "Like I said, it's good exercise."

She narrowed her gaze. "And it has nothing to do with my…issues with elevators?"

"I may have noticed that you didn't seem particularly comfortable." His awareness surprised her. It had been her experience that people like Steve Nolan, who'd been born to expect others to pay attention to *them*, rarely returned the favor. But he was proving to be very different from what she'd expected, in a lot of ways.

"It's not that I'm afraid or anything," she said.

"I never assumed that was the case." He didn't sound patronizing, and she let out a long breath.

She was being overly paranoid about the germs thing. It wasn't like her father even wanted her by his side, anyway. But she still had hope that he would change his mind, and when he finally asked for her, if she'd caught something and didn't realize it, or was sick and couldn't go to him…

She swallowed the sudden lump in her throat, and she swallowed the urge to explain her fears to Nolan.

She didn't say anything the rest of the way down the stairs.

They took her car since he still didn't have a rental, but Steve didn't mind. She drove with as much competence as she did everything else, and he liked watching her. He liked that she could probably kick his ass, and that she had no problem telling him off, too. He liked that she had enough confidence to choose a blue dress, even though he'd suggested a black one. He liked her independence, her intelligence, her grit, and fire. The stiff and professional bodyguard he'd first met was still there, but now it was just another facet of a puzzle he was becoming desperate to solve.

All these years, he'd been trying to give his family back the kind of life that had been ripped from them when his father died. If he continued the way he was going—the way he'd always planned—Optimus Inc. would go global before the end of the year. He'd probably be engaged to a socialite just as fast. His mother would reclaim her place at the country club, and his sister would have her pick of rich, successful young men. He could be the man that his father had failed to be.

It should have been enough. He looked at April Porter. Why wasn't it enough for him now?

At the club, they split up to change. Leo was waiting for him in the ring when he came out onto the floor, bouncing on the balls of his feet with a hard look on his face.

"We've got to stop doing this after you've had a bad day." Steve groaned.

"Come on, tough guy. You can handle it."

He grinned and got in the ring.

April was waiting for him when he finished his sparring match, and both he and Leo climbed down. She'd dressed in her gym attire with a pair of gloves tied by the laces over one shoulder and a towel over the other, but his fierce protector was in full bodyguard mode, sticking close with her eyes peeled for danger.

"Not bad." Leo clapped him on the shoulder. "I think you almost gave me a bruise this time." He had miles of experience and was just razzing Steve. "See you on Monday?" he called.

"I'll let you know." He started stripping off his gloves.

As Leo headed for the locker room, Steve tossed the gloves on the bench and collapsed there, draping his towel over the back of his neck.

"The two of you are pretty evenly matched," April offered.

"No matter how many hours I put in, I can't get a leg up on him." He shook his head, taking deep breaths. "I thought I finally had him on that last move, but he danced out of the way like he saw me coming a mile away."

"That's because he did," she said.

He looked up at her. She stood at attention beside him, looking so gorgeous he could barely hold himself back. All he wanted to do was throw her down on the canvas and do wicked things to her with his hands and his tongue.

"It's not your speed or your strength that's the problem."

He hadn't been able to get the taste of her out of his mind. Every little thing she did made him want to kiss her again. She chewed her bottom lip right now and he was *this close* to pulling her down onto his lap. "David can always take down Goliath with just one shot, as long as it's the right shot. But you're so eager to throw as many punches as you can, you're never going to have the right shot."

He'd actually gotten similar advice before. "But he's relentless. There's no time to hold back and wait for an opening that will never come. I've got to get in there and make my own opening."

She shook her head. "Boxing isn't about who can be the most aggressive." There was a dark look in her eyes as she said it, as if the tip had conjured a memory for her.

"You sound as if that was a lesson you learned the hard way."

She glanced down and visibly swallowed, but said nothing. Nope. She still wouldn't let him in.

He told himself it was too soon but couldn't help the stab of disappointment that speared him in the gut.

"A pro will tell you that a match is all about strategy," she said. "It takes as much planning and preparation as anything else. You have to study, so that you know exactly what your opponent's going to do *before* you get in the ring with him. And then it isn't a matter of waiting for openings or pushing back, because you've worked out the entire fight from beginning to end before it even starts. No matter what he does, you can keep steering him where you want him until it's time for that final shot, the one that takes him down."

He soaked in her advice, but at the same time, he wanted to take the bottom lip she kept chewing on between his teeth and run his tongue across it. But then she would stop talking, and when she spoke it was like being bathed in sunlight. She could tell him that an ice storm was on the way, and he would still melt.

"Everybody has a tell, and if you can figure out what your adversary's are, then you use them against him. For example, you have a tendency to project your moves with a double step, especially your right cross. In fact, Leo's shoulders tensed up every time you did it, so he obviously recognized it, and he was able to counter every time."

He grinned. "Is that all?"

She hesitated. "Well…"

He chuckled.

She shrugged, drawing back a step with a crease in her brow. "It's nothing, never mind. I didn't mean to—"

He leaned forward and grabbed her hand to keep her from backing away. The contact shocked them both. Each of them drew in a short breath and froze in place.

When she would have extracted her hand from his, he squeezed. "I have an honest to goodness professional boxer offering me advice on my technique, and you better believe I'm going to suck every drop of knowledge out of her."

Her cheeks went pink as if he'd offered to suck something else from her.

Damn. And now that's *exactly* what he was thinking of, and he wasn't going to get it out of his head until he got her alone.

"You throw too much weight in front of your lead step. It makes you vulnerable, because in that moment it wouldn't take much to send you toppling off balance with the right nudge." She cleared her throat and glanced down at his hand still clasping hers. "You know, I could maybe give you some pointers. If you wanted me to, I mean." She shook her head almost before the words were completely out of her mouth. "Sorry, you don't need… That's presumptuous of me, and—"

He stopped her before she could take back the offer and

stood up to look into her eyes. "Yes."

She blushed even deeper, but nodded. "Okay." He pulled the towel off her shoulder and draped it across the bench. Her gaze snapped up. "Uh, now?"

"Have you got somewhere better to be?" he asked with a smile.

"Not if you don't."

Her response didn't satisfy him like he'd thought it would. Was he still *just* an assignment to her? There would come a time when it was no longer her job to be with him, and then what would her response be to that same question?

But he wasn't going to be asking that question once this was all over. He was going to move on and seize the future he'd been planning for ten years, like it never happened. He was going to focus on giving his family the lifestyle they deserved.

Chapter Eight

April stood under the spray of water as she showered in the club's locker room. She and Nolan had sparred together for about an hour, the best hour she could remember spending in a long time. Not too many guys would have been able to take boxing instruction from a woman, but his confidence shone from him like a beacon, and she quickly realized he wasn't really taking her advice because he needed it. He was more than capable of analyzing his own weaknesses and hammering them into strengths. He had entered the ring with her because he enjoyed it, and Steve Nolan didn't deny himself anything that would bring him pleasure.

That should have been just one more reason for her to keep her distance, but being with him, she didn't think about death, germs, her career, her past, or anything else. He was like a force of nature, overwhelming her senses with his vitality and intensity, and all her worries stayed on the other side of those ropes. She had no choice but to focus on him completely.

A dangerous activity. Watching him move, watching the

sweat trickle over every bulge of muscle, watching him watch her. More than once, the tips she'd opened her mouth to tell him floated away from her like all of her good intentions, and all the reasons why falling for him was a bad idea seemed unimportant.

He turned out to be a great partner, except for the fact that he'd refused to hit her. She'd egged him on, but he hadn't budged. They danced around each other, and she gave him a few tips her dad had taught her back in the day, but whenever she came at him, he dodged and faked, and if it looked like she wouldn't be able to evade a hit, he'd always pulled the punch.

When she'd climbed out of the ring, she had been breathing heavily, her entire body singing, her blood pumping. But not just because of the workout. Even now, she still hadn't cooled off, even under the icy spray of water.

She turned off the shower and quickly dressed. But this time, Nolan was the one waiting for her when she came back out fifteen minutes later.

He'd changed back into his new jeans and sweater. It should be a sin for someone to look so good and so laid-back at the same time. He leaned against the post with his arms crossed , and his gaze turned scorching as she approached. "You have no idea the trouble I get into when left to my own devices," he said in a low voice when she stopped in front of him. "Ten minutes waiting with nothing to do but imagine you naked in the showers, and I was this close to going in there and joining you."

She hissed and looked around, but thankfully, they were alone. She understood by now that he thrived on unsettling people and she couldn't take anything he said seriously, but her heart pounded despite the reminder. "You're horrible. Why can't you be serious just once?"

His eyes flared with challenge. He pulled away from the

post and came closer. He traced the line of her jaw with his finger. "You're not ready for me to be serious," he murmured.

They stopped to pick up Nolan's tuxedo for the gala. Luckily, it had been at the drycleaner's and not his apartment, or it probably would have been slashed along with the rest of his clothes.

When they got back to his place, John was already there, waiting in the hall by Nolan's front door. He nodded hello as they passed. April had insisted on some added backup for the gala tonight. Posing as Nolan's date would keep her close to him, but now that the incidents had escalated into violence, she'd suggested to her boss that they should also have eyes on the sidelines to watch the crowd. The head of their agency was a good friend of April's from college. When April went to Quantico, Nora had taken over her father's security company, where she'd met John—now her husband and business partner—and she'd agreed with April.

April hung back at the front door to make it clear she wasn't staying. "What time do you want me to return in order to leave for the event tonight?"

"Don't worry about it. I'll pick you up," he said. Nolan hadn't been overly impressed with the idea of more bodyguards, but surprisingly, he hadn't argued with her. He seemed a little preoccupied, though. Was he having second thoughts about not having a real date?

She grimaced. "That's probably not a good idea. It wouldn't be—"

"Professional? I asked you out on a date, which means I get to be the one in charge of the details."

"Not a real date," she reminded him. She should keep reminding herself as well, because it was all too easy to envision herself on his arm as he looked down at her with the promise of what would come afterward gleaming from his eyes.

He grinned. "If we're going to fool anyone, we've got to treat it like a date."

"Fine, but you're the client. You shouldn't have to drive all the way out to Brooklyn when I could just come—"

His voice lowered. "April, if it doesn't involve a security issue, you will not be calling the shots tonight. Do you understand that?"

She opened her mouth to object, but his expression turned dark. He stepped forward. Unprepared and unnerved, she took a corresponding step back. Her shoulder blades hit the closed door. His hand flattened against it, trapping her there between the wood...and a hard place.

"Tonight you are going to enjoy yourself. You are even going to let me get to know you." He dipped his head.

"I am?" she croaked. A rush of goose bumps rose in response to the provocation of his hot breath against the too-sensitive skin at her nape, right there just beneath her ear.

"You are," he promised. She felt his mouth twitch against the column of her neck. He was smiling.

A shiver of anticipation shook her.

"Do you think you can loosen that ironclad grip you've got on yourself long enough to do that?"

She swallowed hard. She was a control freak. Lately, so much had spiraled out of her control—including her father's illness and her own future—that she hated the idea of willingly giving up any of the things she *could* control.

"Why?"

"Why what?"

"Why do you care about getting to know me? Another few days and I'll be out of your life again, anyway."

He nodded, acknowledging without hesitation that their

acquaintance had a short shelf-life. "But we have right here, right now." He punctuated every word with a press of his lips to her neck, starting at her jaw and working his way down to the protrusion of her collarbone. Her legs turned to jelly, and her grip on the door handle tightened until she couldn't feel her fingers. "And there's no reason not to make the most of it."

Could she do it? Could she give herself a free pass and live in the moment for one night? It wouldn't be repeating her past mistakes with Jeremy if she kept her eyes wide open and her heart closed. Besides, she had to admit, she was curious. So far he'd been inappropriate, irreverent, and mostly charming, but what would it be like to get the full-on Steve Nolan charm, the kind of treatment that inspired entire websites to his prowess? Finally, she nodded. "As long as it doesn't compromise your safety, I can agree to a certain level of...intimacy."

"Good. Very good," he murmured. She held her breath and waited for him to kiss her...but he didn't. Abruptly, he drew back, looking like the cat that got the canary. "Then I'll pick you up at eight. Be ready."

She was still thinking about his proposal as she drove up to her father's house, but the sight of the dark windows was sobering. She turned on the hall light as she unlocked the door, turned on the kitchen light on her way through to the living room, and turned on the lights going all the way up the stairs.

It didn't help. The house still felt empty, abandoned. She stood in the doorway of her father's bedroom. The bed was bare, and the drapes had been drawn tight. Even her father's dresser had been cleared of all the stuff he usually piled up on there, like boxing gloves, photos, and cologne, as if he didn't expect to be back. Was this her father's not-so-subtle way of preparing her for the worst? Did he think that if he died there'd be less for her to do if his room had already been stripped clean?

She smothered a sob with a hand over her mouth and turned out the light. Down the hall in her own room, she picked up the phone and called the hospital. The phone rang four times, then five. She was about to give up and run out to the car to race over there and find out what was wrong, when he finally answered.

"Dad?"

"Hey," he said. "What do you want?"

She winced at the abrupt edge to his thin voice. *I want to see you. I want to hold your hand through this. I want you to remember how much I need you and love you.* "Oh, well I thought... I wanted to ask how your treatment went today. How are you feeling?"

"Didn't I tell you this morning that I was fine? You didn't have to call again."

Tears clogged her throat. "Dad, I just—"

"I have to go. The nurse is bringing dinner in now." There was nothing else for such a long moment that April thought he'd simply hung up on her, until finally he said, "Good night, April."

She waited with baited breath, but this time the line had gone dead. "Good night, Dad," she whispered.

When the doorbell rang promptly at eight, she'd pulled herself together. Did being on time mean that Nolan was as anxious about tonight as she was?

She spared a final look in the full-length mirror hanging from the back of her bedroom door and took a deep breath. She hadn't felt this nervous since she and Jeremy had gone to that fancy Italian place uptown.

For the hundredth time, she wondered if agreeing to this had been a mistake.

The bell rang again, and she swore. Too late to back out, but as long as she remembered that Nolan was a successful businessman who was headed for great things, and she was just a bodyguard—his bodyguard—she'd be able to get through one night, and she would just have to re-establish their professional boundaries in the morning.

She hastened down the stairs as quickly as she could in the two-inch heels she hadn't had any other occasion to wear in over a year.

Her breath caught as she pulled the door open to greet him. "Uh, hi."

For the life of her, she couldn't come up with anything else.

It was a gorgeous late-spring evening. Presumably, the stars glittered in the cloudless sky overhead, and if she could breathe, she'd be filled with the scent of daffodils and white magnolias from the neighbor's garden. But the sight of him stripped away everything, even her reason. She struggled to remember her own name as she took him in. The sexy grin. The fresh shave. The devastating breadth of his shoulders in a perfectly cut tuxedo. And the limousine parked at the curb behind him.

She was completely out of her league. The garter holding up her stockings felt old-fashioned. She felt the straps against her legs like they were made of iron. The dress itself was beautiful, and she had no doubt that it looked great on her... which suddenly made her feel like a fraud. Nolan looked completely natural all dressed up, but she'd been practicing walking in these shoes for an hour before getting dressed, just to make sure she wouldn't trip over herself and embarrass him. She'd even debated wearing a pair of ballet flats instead, weighing her responsibility as his bodyguard with her desire to look like she belonged on his arm.

The heels had won out only because her boss Nora had assured her there was going to be enough backup at the event tonight, so she shouldn't have to do any running even if something did happen.

He didn't say anything right away. His appreciative gaze ran the length of her slowly, as if he wanted to savor the moment. Her whole body tightened in response, from her nipples to her core. Finally, he gazed into her eyes and the sparks bouncing back and forth between them only intensified. "Hi, yourself. You look amazing," he said with the most sincerity she'd ever heard out of him.

She only realized he'd kept one hand behind his back when he pulled it out to hand her the single white rose. She'd never received one before. She loved it. White was simple, clean, and perfect, without the drama of a red rose. "Thank you," she whispered.

He held out his arm.

She turned to grab her clutch and lock the door behind her, then let him lead her down the walk. She giggled as John got out of the driver's seat of the limo and came around to open the door for them, with a deadpan look on his face.

"What's so funny?" He threw her a bemused look, which only made her giggle harder as she slid onto the buttery leather seat.

She waited until he'd followed her in and the door closed. The glass divider between the front and back seats was already in place, so they were basically alone. The car was huge, but Nolan didn't give her any space. Instead of sitting on the bench opposite her, he sat right beside her so their thighs touched.

"This reminds me a little too much of my senior prom." She looked around and grinned. "But you're not Tommy Morrison, and I'm not wearing yards of poufy pink chiffon and an orchid wrist corsage the size of my forearm."

He laid his arm across the back of the seat and smiled. "Somehow, I can't envision either the boxing spitfire April Porter, or the investigative genius April Porter, decked out in pink chiffon." He snapped his fingers. "And I also can't believe I forgot to pick up a corsage."

She laughed and let herself relax into the seats. "That's not a sight anyone is ever going to see," she said. "Only my father has a copy of those photos, and I've been assured that they're locked up tight against the light of day."

Her hand clenched in her lap as she mentioned Dad. Nolan noticed. God, he noticed everything. "How is your father?" he asked.

"Fine. He's doing fine." She plastered on a smile and changed the subject. "So, who did you go to the prom with?"

A moment of disappointment flashed across his face, but it was gone before she could even be sure that's what she saw. "I didn't go at all," he admitted with a casual shrug.

"Don't tell me a guy who looks this hot in a suit couldn't get a date?"

"There wasn't always so much of this." He showed off a cheeky flex of his bicep. "I *was* a pretty hard-core math geek once, remember?" He was still smiling, but the smile no longer went to his eyes. "Besides, my birthday was right around that time, and…" He trailed off and glanced over her shoulder out the window.

A lightbulb suddenly went on. "Oh, jeez," she said with a gasp. "That's about the same time your father…"

"Killed himself," he finished in a stone-cold voice. "In the house. With my birthday party going on right downstairs. In the circumstances, it seemed in poor taste to attend the prom a week later."

She put her hand on his arm. "I'm so sorry."

"It was a long time ago."

Maybe, but she knew well that time could never completely heal those kinds of wounds.

Her mother's death hadn't been as dramatic or public, but it had been tragic all the same, and it had shaken her to the core. April was still haunted by those final days, by the gaunt shell that her lively, beautiful mother had become at the end. And she regretted all the things she'd never gotten to say, and all the things they'd never do together.

Thinking about it now made her angry with her father for pushing her away when they needed all the time they could get with one another.

"Wait a minute." She paused to connect the dots as she recalled the news stories she'd been reading yesterday about the incident and looked up at Nolan. "That means your birthday is…"

"Next week," he admitted with a clenched jaw. "But it's not really something I go out of my way to acknowledge these days."

They spent a few moments in silence after that. The backseat of the limo seemed to get smaller as both of their pasts piled on in to join the party.

"Well," he said with a wince and a chuckle. "This is a sorry start to our first date."

The fact that he was calling it a "first" date unnerved her. She'd pretty much convinced herself that this was a one-off fueled by curiosity on both their parts, and when she could think about it in those terms, she'd still felt safe and in control.

In fact, she'd been expecting him to lay a practiced seduction technique on her pretty quick, proving he thought of her the same as all his other women, but so far he'd been a complete gentleman.

"So tonight…why did your mother decide to combine your father's memorial with a charity event?" she asked, clasping her hands in her lap to keep them to herself. The temptation of Nolan's proximity was so distracting she could barely focus on the conversation.

He nodded. "She's on the board for the organization, and she *hated* the idea of anyone patting her hand and whispering false condolences on the anniversary of my father's death. She decided to turn it into something productive instead."

"That's a wonderful way to approach it. From what I read today, this thing is going to be the event of the season. You must be proud of her." April had spent the afternoon reviewing the in-house security arrangements with the venue staff and making plans to beef it up where necessary, to keep Nolan safe. It had relieved her mind to learn that everything was already very organized. "Your family went through a lot, but she sounds like an amazingly strong, resilient woman." *Like you,* she wanted to add, but that would have betrayed just how much she'd been thinking about him beyond what a bodyguard should think about her client.

She winced. He hesitated so long that she was sure she'd stepped over the line. He'd made it more than clear that he didn't like to discuss his personal life, and asking after one's mother was definitely venturing into personal territory.

"It's okay, I didn't mean to pry. I respect your boundaries, and I would never—"

"After my father's death, my mother retreated from the city and all the social connections she had here. It was too painful for her to face those people, and it took a long time before she wanted to return. But now that she finally has, she refuses to hide from our past. Instead, she wants to use what happened to help others with similar problems."

"You're very lucky to have someone like her as a role model," April murmured, her throat tight as she thought of her own mother.

"She and my sister are the reason I started Optimus Inc. with Harrison." She was struck numb by the tenderness that crept into his smile when he spoke of his family. He obviously had a soft spot that couldn't be diluted by his typical insouciance, and she found it endearing and completely irresistible.

She cleared her throat. "Your family lost a lot. A husband, a father, a provider."

"It was hard on them," he admitted, glancing out the dark tinted windows.

Her heart squeezed. *It was hard on you.*

She wondered if he realized that she could see the reflection of his solemn expression in the window; that his carefree, impudent mask had slipped to reveal the pain he still carried with him. "You wanted to help your family get back their security and their pride."

He turned back to her. "Yes, but mostly I just couldn't stand the looks of pity from people who'd pretended to be our friends. I couldn't stand being labeled and ashamed of something I had no control over, so I resolved to make sure they could never pity me again."

"Well, you've definitely managed to turn all that around. The press loves you, and your family is climbing back to the top of that social ladder." *All he needed was a stunning, equally connected wife.*

His mouth thinned. "And I refuse to let anything happen to jeopardize that."

She shook off her disappointment. He hadn't seemed like the type to find wealth and social status so important, but after spending the last two days together, she understood why they would be. The playboy persona was just a mask—and not a very good one for anyone who'd spent even a few hours with him. Nolan assumed responsibility for his family at an early age, and he would never fail them, because he cared...and she thought he probably couldn't bear the thought of being likened to his father.

His inflexible position regarding the situation with the anonymous threats made more sense now, too. Nolan hated for anyone to have control over any part of his life. The fact that he'd let her intervene as much as he had was actually pretty surprising. She had a feeling that determination came from the same place as his resolute desire to master the art of boxing as well.

She'd been wrong before. Except for the fact that they were both accomplished and connected, Nolan wasn't anything like Jeremy. Yes, he was from that world, and yes, he was charming. He was flirtatious. But those traits were backed by a genuineness that her ex had lacked. Behind Nolan's playboy antics was a deeply motivated man.

No, he might not be like Jeremy, but his drive and ambition made him even more untouchable to someone like her, because Nolan was headed for great things, and if he did finally settle down, he was going to need someone who could play the game just as well as he did. April knew she was not that person.

The car slowed, and April looked out the window. "We're here," she said. The event was being held at the Met.

She shifted to the seat closer to the front and tapped on the glass. It slowly slid open, and John twisted around in the passenger seat to grin at her. "What can I do for you, ma'am?"

She reached through and punched him on the arm. "First of all, you can quit ma'aming me." She turned serious. "Everything's in place?"

He tapped his ear, indicating that Nora was on point at the other end. April was also wearing a mic and an earpiece, but in order to maintain a semblance of privacy, she wasn't being patched into the main feed. Nora would be able to hear everything she was saying, but April would only get an earful if there was a security emergency.

"Two of our guys are making extra rounds at all the entrances, as per your suggestion," said John. "And there'll be another three inside on the floor, including me."

That had been the original plan, but she was glad to have confirmation. "Good. That should be enough."

He nodded and turned to Nolan. "Sir, please remain in the vehicle until we give the all clear."

The window closed again. "Are you sure all this is necessary?" Nolan asked.

"Given the rapid escalation of the incidences of violence against you, we need to take greater precautions when you're out in public."

"But this is a pretty busy place. Only a nutcase is going to try something in a room full of people, at a charity event no less."

She raised her brows. "And you think we're *not* dealing with a crazy person because…?"

He laughed. "I guess you have a point."

"The museum has good security, but I identified a few weaknesses in their program and just want to make sure everything gets covered properly. We can't afford to be lax," she reminded him.

He reached out and pulled her back across the space to the seat right beside him. His arm slipped around her waist, and suddenly the shadowy car seemed as intimate as a darkened hotel room. She'd been focused on his safety only a moment ago, but now his mouth was a mere inch from hers, and she couldn't think of anything else.

"I love when you talk security to me," he murmured in a low voice, making her stomach flutter.

A day after meeting Nolan, she knew. She *knew* she was in trouble. It was crazy how much he affected her.

She couldn't deny the spark between them, but neither could she ever forget that they were completely wrong for each other. Even if their jobs, their position, and their futures weren't in conflict, neither of them were ready for a relationship. Nolan was focused on his company, and she needed to focus on her father. Tonight was just business.

Chapter Nine

When April had opened her door to him, he'd experienced a moment of true speechlessness; and Nolan always had something to say...usually something antagonizing or provoking. This time, though, he hadn't been able to bring himself to say anything but the absolute, unvarnished truth. She was gorgeous, and he'd wanted her to know it.

She still hadn't let her hair down, even for an evening like this. That was the first thing he'd noticed. The high, sleek bun only gave her the timeless beauty of Grace Kelly and exaggerated the stubborn tilt of her chin and the fire in her eyes. The dress she'd bought was a perfect choice. It was understated but cut to highlight every curve. She'd put on just a hint of makeup, enough to add some smoke and mystery to her already striking features. A powerful combination that left him dizzy with lust, which might prove to be awkward when they danced...and they *would* dance. He'd have it no other way.

The crowd was thickest near the entrance, and even as he put his arm around April to shield her, she shifted to put herself directly between him and everyone who looked as if they might be approaching them.

He could have told her that none of these people were dangerous. These were the people he'd grown up with. Silly, rich, bored. They were here tonight, and they would be at the next event tomorrow, and the one after that, because there was nothing of actual substance to their social butterfly lives.

As a teenager, Steve had imagined that adulthood would consist of party after party, with the occasional business lunch thrown in, and an endless string of beautiful women. It had seemed reasonable to assume given the example provided by his father, who had thrived in just this kind of environment. But then everything had fallen apart, and the same men who'd played golf with Robert Nolan, drank with Robert Nolan, and worked with Robert Nolan, had started talking about how they'd always known he was unstable and it was no surprise that he couldn't manage his own company. They'd told their wives not to invite his wife to their homes and told their children not to play with his son and daughter. The man who'd never spent an evening alone in life had been lowered into the ground with less than fifteen mourners at his funeral, including his devastated family.

At first, Steve had tried to change their minds. He'd begged and pleaded for his friends to stand by him, watched his mother and sister cry too many times. But it hadn't taken long to figure out how the world really worked, and he'd become determined that no one would ever see that weakness in him ever again. He'd worked hard to maintain the image of a carefree playboy, knowing it was the best way to make these people forget about how broken and shattered he'd once felt.

Some would say he'd succeeded too well. No one outside of his immediate circle—which included his mother and sister, Ben Harrison and his fiancée, and Meredith—knew who the real Steve Nolan was today.

Ironically, the only other person he knew as intensely private as he was would be April Porter. She was reserved and defensive, nothing like the venomous, superficial people he had become used to.

As they stepped into the wide foyer of the museum, Steve noticed the first of April's extra security personnel, and it didn't take long to pick out the rest. He was used to making a production of entrances, but this was a little ridiculous. Too many nondescript black suits; dudes pressing their index finger to their ears and whispering, apparently to no one.

Someone was going to notice, probably the press. And as soon as that happened, the shit was going to hit the fan. Ben was already worried. He'd called in a panic just before Steve had gone to pick up April. Apparently this morning's incident had been leaked to the most shameless rag on the net, *Daily Scoop*, which meant it had gone from a single slashed tire story to death threats painted in pig's blood across his windshield.

Steve had briefly considered cancelling, but he and Ben both agreed that he needed to be visible tonight to prove to the world—and the large number of their local shareholders that would be in attendance at the gala—that he wasn't running scared, everything was under control, and they didn't have to worry about putting their money into Optimus Inc.

He and April hadn't taken more than ten steps through the crowd when someone called his name. "Brace yourself," he murmured.

"What? Why?" April immediately went into bodyguard mode. She stiffened, at full attention as she scanned everyone's faces.

He put a quelling hand on her arm and chuckled. "Terrorists are not about to descend," he said. "But almost as distressing…my mother is bearing down on us."

Her mouth dropped open as if that was indeed distressing. She smoothed a hand over her hip. "It won't be that bad," he promised. "As long as you don't show any fear, she can't steal your soul."

She glared at him. "Are you *never* serious?"

"It's bad for the colon. You should keep that in mind, you know." He grinned then turned to face the approaching woman. "Mother! What a surprise to see you here."

She smiled like the cat that caught the canary as she looked up at April and leaned in to kiss Steve's cheek. No air kisses for his mother. No, she planted both lips full on him, leaving a lipstick mark that he'd have to rub away as soon as she left.

"I organized this; you knew very well I would be here. If anyone should be surprised, it's me." Her gaze narrowed in April's direction. "You showed less than no interest in this event when I asked you to come."

"And I still have no interest in it," he admitted with a tight-lipped expression, but he squeezed her hand. "But I do have this crazy interest in checking in on you every once in a while."

His mother beamed, and it was nice to see her happy. She'd shed too many tears since her husband's death, but now that she'd finally returned from her self-imposed exile, she laughed a lot more, and she seemed to be having no trouble re-forging the society connections that had snapped ten years ago through no fault of her own. Steve only wished that she and Grace would let go of the past completely. He couldn't bring himself to understand the point of a memorial service for a selfish, stupid man who'd destroyed his family and then taken his own life. There must be some other way to bring much-needed recognition to a worthy charity.

She kissed his cheek again.

"Cut it out. My date is going to get jealous," he teased, rubbing his cheek.

As if she'd been waiting for the opening, his mother said,

"And are you going to introduce us?"

"April Porter, ma'am. I'm pleased to meet you." Like a drill sergeant, she sharply stuck out her hand. His mother looked down at it with a bemused expression before accepting the offering, and they shook hands—probably more vigorously than his mother had expected.

"I'm Sarah Nolan," she answered, giving April an up-and-down look of assessment. She knew him well and understood that while the paparazzi might have caught him with a couple of bimbos in the past, he wouldn't have dared bring someone to a public event being run by his mother without thinking long and hard about it first. "So, Ms. Porter, do I know that name?"

"I'm sorry, I-I don't think we've met before." April looked a little lost, but Steve understood exactly what was going on.

He leveled his mother with a hard look. That might be the typical first question out of every other matchmaking mama—is the girl's family good enough?—but she knew better than to judge people by such false qualifications. Her own husband had come from the finest New York stock, with a lineage that went back generations, and look how that had turned out.

She'd seen the warning in his eyes and backed down...a little. "Well then, how did the two of you meet?"

"Oh, well, I'm..." She looked to him, uncertain what to say.

He swore under his breath. He should have warned his mother ahead of time, but he wouldn't lie to her now. "She's my bodyguard," he admitted quietly.

Her socially polite expression turned to one of shock and fear. "Bodyguard? Steven, do you want to explain why you need a *bodyguard*?"

Shit. "It's no big deal, but I should have called you, and I meant to but the time got away from me. I'm sorry. I'll tell you about it tomorrow, okay?"

"What kind of trouble are you in?" Her voice had gotten very thin.

"No trouble," he assured her firmly. He was the one to kiss her on the cheek this time, silently pleading with her to let it go. "Everything's fine, I promise."

She looked slightly appeased, but a frown line creased her forehead. "I'll expect your call *first thing* in the morning."

He raised his right hand. "Bright and early, hangover or no."

A gentleman wearing a headset who appeared to belong to the museum appeared at his mother's side and tapped her on the shoulder with a subtle clearing of his throat. She squeezed her eyes shut and sighed before pasting on a smile that looked much less natural than before he'd spilled the beans, and he only blamed himself.

"Hey, I know you have work to do tonight, so we'll be on our way," he told her. "Don't worry about anything, okay?"

She nodded, but the shadows in her eyes didn't go away, and he knew she was reliving the night a gunshot had rung out through the house and she'd run into her own bedroom and found her husband's blood splashed all over the walls. The night she'd realized everything had been falling apart around her for months and Robert had kept her completely in the dark until it was way too late.

He hated that he'd scared her and made her feel the same way as she had that day. When she squeezed his hand one last time and disappeared back into the crowd, he heaved a sigh of regret.

Blinking, he looked around at all the lights and decorations. "I should have told her that everything looked great. Do you think she wants me to tell her that everything looks great?"

April put her hand on his arm. "It does look great, and

I'm sure she knows it. I'm so sorry, Nolan. I froze when your mother asked who I was. I should have come up with something instead of putting you in that position."

He shook his head. "It's my fault. I should have told her what was going on sooner. I kept putting it off because I didn't want her to worry."

He looked down and realized he had her hand in a grip so tight her fingers must have gone numb, but she hadn't said a word. He let go abruptly. "I'll talk to her and my sister tomorrow."

"I can have our guys keep an eye on her for the balance of the evening," she suggested. "So far, we've had no reason to believe that the attacks against you have any possibility of extending to your family, but I'll suggest we keep some light surveillance on Mrs. Nolan and your sister until we're certain that the matter is resolved."

He hadn't wanted to admit that this whole thing might touch them, but he couldn't risk it a minute longer. He nodded. "Thanks."

Her mouth dropped open. "What was that? Did you just accept my professional judgment? Did you just say thank you?"

He really had been an asshole.

She turned her head and murmured in a low voice, talking into a microphone, arranging protection for his mother right away. The idea that he needed April and her agency to protect him and his family still drove him insane, but he realized just how grateful he was to have her.

The crowd was getting to him. The laughter and clinking of glassware had become abrasive. He needed to move, and this was no place for a boxing match.

He slipped his arm around his bodyguard's waist and smiled when she let out a gasp of surprise. "I think it's time to dance," he murmured in her ear.

"Ah, wouldn't you like to make the rounds first, or get a drink?"

"Do you need a drink?" he asked.

"I don't drink when I'm on the job."

"I thought you were on a date."

"I might have to agree with you," she teased with a grin. "After all, I met your mother and everything."

"And how many other guys have introduced you to their parents?"

She pursed her lips and shook her head, eyes sparkling like they were made of stars. "I'm not telling you that."

"Well, at the moment, I have absolutely no interest in alcohol, or mingling." He gazed into them and was mesmerized. "Or anything else but you. Don't make me wait any longer to hold you in my arms. That's the only reason we're still here."

Her eyes flashed as she glowered up at him, making her even more bewitching. "Your mother was right, wasn't she? You had no intention of coming to this thing at all, did you?"

He shrugged. "I won't deny that the temptation to get you all decked out and show you my moves was definitely a deciding factor."

She raised a sculpted eyebrow, but he recognized the playful smile tugging at her mouth. "Your moves?"

With a chuckle, he steered her into the Great Hall. Tables had been set up along the perimeter and the wait at the bar was long and three lines deep, but they were headed for the center of the almost deserted dance floor. The alcohol hadn't been flowing long enough yet for most people to drum up enough bravery for dancing. April herself suddenly looked nervous, glancing over her shoulder as if marking the nearest exit.

He stopped and let go of her, but held out his arm in invitation.

"Maybe we should—"

"Dance with me, April Porter." His voice lowered. "Here. Now."

To his surprise, she took a deep breath and closed the distance between them. She laid one hand on his forearm and the other in his open palm, but as the band started to play a modern waltz she stiffened almost immediately. Panic lit her eyes and she bit her lip harder than usual.

With a soft smile, he ducked his head to whisper in her ear. "There's nothing to it. Just follow my lead."

Heat exploded in her cheeks the moment he realized she didn't know how to dance.

"I'm sorry," she muttered, drawing back. "This isn't going to work. We should probably just stop before I embarrass—"

He tipped her chin up and smiled into her face. "It's easy. If you can dance around an opponent in the boxing ring, you can do this," he promised.

April was completely out of her element, and she couldn't pretend otherwise any longer. This place, these people…it wasn't her. Champagne and dancing, dresses and small talk. Life with her rough and tumble father in a dusty boxing club hadn't prepared her for this. Of all the disgusting things Jeremy had said about her to his buddies, he'd been right about that.

She caught a glimpse of John across the room, looking completely inconspicuous. *That* was her. She lived on the sidelines of these people's lives…and it was completely fine. She'd never wanted anything more.

Until now.

Is this really the kind of life she wanted? *No.* It wasn't the fancy party or dressing up that made her heart race. It was *him.* Steve Nolan. Just *him.*

Despite his past, he walked through this stuck-up crowd

like he owned it…and she had absolutely no doubt that before long, he would. It was easy to see that Nolan was destined for great things, and if she was going to spend any amount of time with him above and beyond the parameters of this particular assignment, these types of events were going to become a regular occurrence.

Good thing there was no chance of that happening.

She glanced over his shoulder. There were a few people milling about on the fringes of the dance floor. One guy wearing a trench coat who turned away before she could catch a glimpse of his face, a couple who swayed to the music as if they were seconds away from joining in the dancing, too, and others who were more interested in the conversation than the music.

Thank God, nobody seemed to care what she and Nolan were doing. Her colleagues watching on the sidelines already knew that her cover was as Nolan's date for the night, so she wouldn't have to worry they would think she was acting unprofessional…even if she totally was.

But since it was clearer than ever that what they had between them was short-lived, she wanted to live every moment of it to the fullest.

He tipped her chin again, silently demanding her full attention, daring her to leave doubt and insecurities at the door.

She nodded. "Let's hope you're Fred Astaire, because that's the only way we're going to look good out on this dance floor." She smiled nervously.

His gaze flared. "You're irresistible. You could stand here without moving a muscle and every guy in this place would still want to cut in on me…but I'm not going to let them," he promised.

His arm curled around her waist. Instead of holding their clasped hands out at arm's length, he tucked them up against his chest and pulled her closer so their bodies were in continual contact all the way down to her thighs. Anticipation and desire coursed through her veins, warming her from her fingertips to her toes.

He grinned. "What is it?" she asked.

He bent forward and whispered in her ear, "Don't look now, but you're dancing."

It was true. She'd been caught by the intent look in his eyes for the last several minutes and hadn't even realized that he was slowly but expertly guiding her across the floor. Her hand rested on his arm, and he covered her fingers with his and tucked her other hand against his chest as they moved together. His heartbeat was strong and steady, calming her nervousness but heightening her awareness of him.

God, he was hot—the kind of hot that melted her bones and left her overwhelmed and dizzy with need. He made her feel graceful, feminine, and desired. She swayed, letting the music penetrate deeper until the moment extended into forever and there was nothing between them but anticipation and promise. It was intoxicating, like sultry tendrils of delicate smoke that weaved around their legs and pulled them closer.

The music changed, and she realized there were quite a few more people on the floor with them now. She glanced over Nolan's shoulder, something was twinging her instincts. She sharpened her gaze but Nolan noticed what she was doing and chuckled. "You can't clock out for even one evening, can you?"

She bit her lip. "I'm sorry, I just have to—"

"It's okay. I kind of like that you're so committed to your work. After all, *I* am your work."

If she was *really* committed, she wouldn't be here pretending to be someone she wasn't, a part of her whispered. She'd be dressed in her ugly suit, watching from the other side of the room while Nolan danced with someone else, maybe the leggy redhead from the restaurant, or the woman who'd called his cell phone while they were in the store, Meredith.

The song ended, and they stopped dancing, but he didn't let her go, not immediately.

Her whole body hummed, and she forgot all about where they were, the clothes that made her feel like an imposter, and even her job. She drowned in the unspoken promises he made with his touch and his gaze, sliding her hands up the lapels of his jacket and around the nape of his neck almost against her will.

His eyes sparkled as he moved to guide her off the dance floor, his smoldering attention fixed on her to the exclusion of all else.

It happened so fast. A movement out of the corner of her eye as she looked up at Nolan, a figure on an intercept course with them as they departed the dance floor. Trench coat. She'd noticed him earlier, but now she was seeing him from the front instead of the back. It was the same man who'd been watching them through the storefront window, the same man from the hotel surveillance video.

He was fixated on Nolan and pushed his way through the few people between them. When he stuffed his hand in his pocket, she reacted instinctively, throwing herself in front of Nolan. Her ankle twisted in her heels, and she slipped across the glossy marble floor. She held on to her balance with a grimace and yelled for backup.

Nolan didn't drop back behind her. He tried to get around her, his face a mask of fury as he locked onto the man still advancing toward them.

"Nolan!" the man called out. He sounded frantic and desperate, and a desperate man wasn't someone she wanted anywhere near her client.

She grabbed Nolan's forearm. "Come on!" A crowd gathered even as trench coat man was taken down, and she yanked Nolan out of the fray, nudging him in front of her as she directed them out of the museum. Even at the main doors, she could hear the man still yelling after them.

"Where are we going?" Nolan snapped.

"John and his crew can handle things back there. You're *my* responsibility, and I have to get you out of here."

He tugged back. "What about my mother?"

April tapped the mic in her ear and asked Nora, who quickly filled her in. "My guy is still with her. She's absolutely safe." She turned back to him and added, "And the assailant is already in custody. My boss is in cooperation with the police—already en route—and we'll have some answers as soon as possible."

They reached the car. Obviously, there was a different driver waiting for them because John was inside the museum, but she recognized him, and so she pushed Nolan into the backseat while he returned to the driver's side door.

"If the situation is in hand, why are we leaving? I need to find out who that is and why the hell he's been attacking me."

She followed Nolan into the car and shut the door. "Drive," she called and tapped on the glass separating the front and back seats. "I'm sorry, but we're staying out of the way. I can't take the chance that this incident might have been a setup."

He frowned and glanced out the window. The city lights on the other side were softened by the tinted glass. "You think this could have been a diversion, so yet *another* attacker could get close to me?"

She shook her head. "I don't actually think that's what was going on. But it wouldn't be the first time, and standard procedure dictates that in the case of a threat to your safety, I get you out immediately, no matter what."

He sighed and collapsed back into the seat. She'd been expecting more of an argument. "Nolan?"

He glanced up and shook his head. "I understand. You're right. I just hope I didn't make your job any harder. I guess I can wait a few more hours to get those answers."

She settled into the soft leather beside him. She let out a sigh and put a hand on his arm. "That was the first time I've had to evacuate one of my charges from a compromised location," she admitted. The adrenaline still had her revved up, and she didn't know what to do about it. "No matter how much training you get, you can never really know how you're going to react when a situation like that actually happens. I think it's a good thing I found out with you."

His frown only deepened. He took her hand and interlaced their fingers together. "I don't know if I like the idea of you being in more situations like that."

She tensed and looked down at their joined hands for a long moment. Unable to speak above a whisper, she said, "If I didn't know better, I'd say that sounded suspiciously like —"

"Like someone who cares about you," he finished.

She sucked in a hiss as he cupped her cheek and bent to kiss her, stealing her breath away along with all the carefully constructed safeguards she'd put in place to keep from falling for him completely.

Her heart was thumping so hard she could hear the echo of it in her ears, feel it all the way down to her toes. His mouth opened over hers, hot and daring and wild. Growing up the way she had, she was no stranger to guys who liked to think they were dangerous. But none of them had been as dangerous as Steve Nolan. And it wasn't his muscles or his attitude — of which he had plenty of both. No, it was what he represented: ambition, power, success. All the things she would never have, all the things that would propel him further away from her over time.

Which is exactly why she'd put those safeguards in place.

And it was exactly the reason they were always destined

to fail.

He pulled her across the seat onto his lap. Her skirt rode up to the tops of her thighs but she didn't care. That only made it easier to throw her leg over his so she was straddling him. It might already be too late for her to come out of this thing at the end of it with her heart intact, but that didn't mean she was going to walk out on the experience altogether. It was too late for that, too.

"Where's your microphone?" he asked in a low voice.

She blinked. The mic? Why did he—

"Can they hear us? Do you *want* them to hear us? Because I could go either way, but I assume…"

Oh. Heat flooded her cheeks. She leaned back enough to reach into the bodice of her dress and remove the small watch battery-shaped mic pinned to the lacy strap of her bra while he watched with a look that said he was eager to get in there himself. She dropped it into her clutch.

"The earpiece?" he asked, pushing the hair back behind her ear, making her blush.

She shook her head. "I can't take that off until you're safely back at home with guards posted at the entrances, but I'm not getting any chatter over the line. We're quiet on the channel unless there's a reason not to be."

He nodded and reached for her again. If she'd thought his kiss was devastating to her senses before, now he shattered her. She curled her arms around his neck and held on tight, shuddering as his hands worked up to the knot in her hair, and his tongue swept her mouth.

She tipped her head slightly. "Don't," she whispered. "Not here." They still had to leave this car and make it to his apartment. She knew it was only an illusion of control, the semblance of propriety, but…

He seemed to understand and left her hair alone. "Jesus, you taste good," he murmured, licking her lips like she was his favorite flavor of ice cream cone. "Like cinnamon and honey and sex."

His hands moved down her back until he spread them over the round cheeks of her ass.

"And just how do I taste like sex?" she asked. Now she was imagining how she *could* taste like sex. It would involve slipping down to her knees between his legs, pulling his zipper down and freeing his cock so she could run her tongue up and down the length of him before sucking him hard and taking him as deep into her mouth as he would fit. Then, afterward, he'd pull her back up to kiss her, and—

"You're warm and wet and sweet, and you suck on my tongue like you never want to let me go." He kissed her again, and when he drew away she followed with a whimper. "Sex, baby. Pure sex. And I can't get enough of it."

She clenched her eyes shut with a groan and let her head fall back. She arched her hips, trying to press her core against him. His lips found the pulse point thrumming madly in her neck, making her gasp with delight, and he slid his hands up her legs from her knees. He found the lace trim at the top of her stockings first and traced it all the way around.

Slowly. Oh so slowly.

Her brain turned to mush when he got to the inside of her thighs, only to make his way back to the clasps of her garters. He flicked them off and kept running his hands up right under the hem of her dress, over her thighs and hips until they circled her waist.

When his finger slipped beneath the string of her thong against her tailbone and followed it down the crack of her ass, she gasped. And when he dipped into the moist heat between her spread legs from behind, she whimpered.

His mouth marked a trail along the cord of her neck, and he tugged both the straps of her dress and her bra off her shoulder to get access to more skin.

She bit her lip to keep from grinding against his fingers. Propriety? What was that? In the back of her mind—way in the back—a voice told her this was not the place to relinquish control. As if to prove it, the car slowed. She swore as she tore her mouth from his. Her pussy pulsed with need. Her breathing was ragged and short.

She glanced out the window. They'd turned onto his street. "We'll be pulling into your building very shortly," she murmured.

He dragged a thumb across her sensitive, bruised lips. "Stay with me tonight," he said.

She nodded. "I'd planned—"

"Not because you think you *should* be there," he clarified, "but because you want to be naked with me all night long."

His focused, direct look reminded her that this was a man who made his own destiny, who was used to getting exactly what he wanted. The fact that he wanted *her*—at least for right now—was heady stuff, but it wasn't the reason why she was going to say yes.

She pulled the strap back up over her shoulder and smoothed her hair before leaning over to kiss him once more. April was going to say yes because she wanted to. It didn't get any plainer or simpler than that.

The car came to a stop. She started to pull back and climb off his lap, but his big hand on the back of her neck kept her close.

"If you stay, I promise to make you scream." He pulled her bottom lip between his teeth playfully.

A sizzle spread through her. Of all her worries, that definitely wasn't it. "A boxer needs to constantly work on his stamina. The way I see it, you asked for a trainer, and I have an obligation to do my very best to put you through your paces," she teased.

Chapter Ten

She straightened her clothes and smoothed her hair to make sure no telling strands had escaped, and by the time the car door opened and he helped her out, there was no sign of the siren that had melted over his fingers and squirmed on his lap. The indomitable Ms. Porter had returned, even if the ugly suit had not.

He hid a smile as she nodded to the driver. He liked the stiff, professional Ms. Porter, especially now that he knew the Amazon was close at hand beneath the surface.

"Hey, Tony. Are we good?" she asked the bodyguard waiting for them in the parking garage. The guy was beefy, with a thick, furrowed brow and a definite bulge in his jacket. He was already holding open the empty elevator, presumably because they hadn't wanted to risk randomly pushing the button with Steve standing there, only to have it open with a gunman waiting to shoot him down.

He shook his head. Was this really the way he'd started to think? Would he be looking for crazed psychos at every street corner now, too?

Tony nodded, giving Steve a once-over. "Nora has cleared your apartment. No word yet as to the identity of the assailant. John went with the officers who transported the guy to the station, but there's an investigator questioning some of the guests at the museum."

"What about Mrs. Nolan?" she said.

"She's been escorted home, and two of our guys are going to stick around outside for the night to keep an eye on things. I understand her daughter is in residence as well, and she has been inquired after. All is well, but she's been asking questions."

"Great. We'll make sure to talk to her first thing in the morning. Thanks so much for your assistance tonight," she said with a friendly smile. The tight ball in Steve's chest relaxed a little. He hadn't realized how worried he'd been about his family until April had made certain to inquire after them. "I guess you're free to go on home. Tell Pete I'm sorry to have kept you out so late on date night."

Tony chuckled and motioned for them to enter the elevator as he said, "I promised to make my Fettuccine Alfredo tomorrow as a compromise, so he's not complaining."

As the elevator door closed, Tony tipped his chin down and murmured something. Steve was fairly certain it was a heads-up to whoever would be waiting for them at the penthouse level.

"You seem to know Tony pretty well," he said.

He wondered if she'd shrug off his question, like she'd done every other time he'd shown a hint of interest in her personal life.

"Not really. I haven't been with the company long, but I knew Tony's partner when I was in training for the FBI. Pete just graduated actually. He got a position in the Virginia office, and he and Tony are going to be moving there in a few weeks. We celebrated last weekend."

She sounded completely genuine in her happiness for the couple, but if he'd been in her place, he probably would have felt at least a *little* melancholy. "You would be celebrating your new post by now, too, if you hadn't left the program, wouldn't you?"

She shrugged. "Then it's definitely better that I left. Even assuming I'd have passed the final tests, there's no guarantee I would have been assigned to an office in the area. And whether or not Dad wants me around right now, I need to be close by…just in case."

Not since that first night sitting on the floor of his wrecked kitchen when she'd told him about her dad's gym had she willingly shared any part of herself with him—and God knew, he'd tried to get her to open up. Not her past, or her present. Not her fears, or her dreams. And yet, he'd discovered things on his own just by watching her and by her own omissions. She'd probably *hate* to know that.

April was perhaps the most aloof person he'd ever met, but in spite of her stubborn walls, he kept finding reasons to admire her. She'd lost her mother as a child, but it hadn't become a crutch. She loved her father and feared for his health. She'd willingly given up her dream of working with the FBI to care for him. She could be happy for her friends' successes even when she felt like she'd been left behind. And she'd approached her assignment to a disrespectful smart-ass with dignity and grace. She was not only beautiful, talented, and whip-smart, but also a class act.

When *his* future had been ripped away by the death of his father, he'd reacted by going through an angry, two-year long rebellion of drinking, partying, and every other vice he could think of before realizing what April had known instinctively: that life wasn't fair and the only way to take control of it was to accept that and just rely on yourself.

The elevator stopped, and the two of them walked out

into the hallway. A woman stood at his doorway and stepped forward. "Mr. Nolan, I'm Nora Shapiro of S & S Security," she said, shaking his hand and sending April a friendly smile. "I wanted to be here in person to bring you up to date on the situation as it currently stands."

He nodded and motioned for the front door. "Why don't you come inside, then?"

She shook her head. "This won't take long, so I'll be brief and leave you to the rest of your evening." She clasped her hands. "The person who approached you at the museum this evening has been identified as Edward Fielding, the son of Justin Fielding."

A chill ran down his spine. The frantic, desperate-looking guy who'd confronted him this evening couldn't have been any older than Steve himself. He'd known Justin Fielding had a son, but none of his investigators had ever been able to locate the family. They'd disappeared along with him and hadn't turned up again, even after news of the car crash.

"Where's his father?" he demanded.

April stepped closer and took his hand, as if to soothe his ruffled feathers. He noticed Nora noticing the gesture, but neither of them said anything about it. Steve, because he was enjoying her touch and didn't want her to realize what she was doing and let go; and Nora, probably because she didn't want to make April feel uncomfortable.

"The police haven't finished their interrogation, but we're on top of the situation and will keep you advised as soon as we know more," Nora said.

Justin Fielding had stolen from his family and destroyed his father. He'd escaped justice all this time while Steve's family had been shamed and blackballed for years afterward. Now that Steve had finally started to put the pieces of their lives back together, the bastard's son thought he could finish what his father started? *Fuck that.*

"I want to be there." His clenched teeth sent pain spiking through his jaw.

The two women shared a telling look. Obviously, they thought that was going to be a bad idea, and maybe they were right. He didn't know if he'd be able to keep his cool if faced with anyone named Fielding, but he didn't much care. "I want answers, and I'm not going to leave it up to the cops to get them. They've spent ten years doing absolutely nothing with this investigation. I have no confidence that even with this guy in their custody, they'll be of any use."

"Police procedure prohibits the public from interrogating a witness, but I'll make some calls in the morning, and we'll see what we can do," April said, squeezing his hand. This time she did realize what she was doing and quickly pulled away. He wanted to reach out and snatch her hand back, but didn't.

"I know a few guys at the station," she said. "Maybe I can pull some strings and at least get us in the same room with him for a minute or two."

Nora stepped aside and moved toward the elevator. "Everything's under control for now. It's getting late, but I should have an agent available to relieve you in about an hour," she said to April.

April blushed and pointedly did *not* look at Steve.

"Send your people home. I think it's safe to say that your company's protection services are no longer required," he said. "The guy's in custody, and I know who he is, if not what he wants. But that's only a matter of time. Ms. Porter's assignment is officially over, don't you agree?"

The woman looked back and forth between him and April. Finally, she nodded. "I understand we will need Mr. Harrison to sign off on the contract to make it official, but I suppose you're right."

April visibly relaxed, and he realized just how much she'd been bothered by the idea of spending the night while "on the job." He was glad it wouldn't be an issue because he wanted nothing between them tonight…nothing at all.

Ms. Shapiro smiled. "I've got some other situations to check on, and a husband to retrieve from the police station, so I'll be going. Email me a report in the morning," she said to April.

April's cheeks were still delightfully pink by the time the elevator door closed on her boss's carefully blank expression, but in every other respect, she'd gone into Ms. Porter mode again, standing very straight and stiff at his side.

Had she changed her mind? It was one thing to get carried away by the shadowed intimacy of the car when his mouth was making her whimper and his fingers delved into her wet warmth, and quite another to stick to that same decision in the cold light of an apartment building hallway after a face-to-face with her boss.

He opened the door and held it for her. She hesitated, and he was positive she would have some reason why she suddenly had to leave. The disappointment almost smothered him, but he bit his tongue. It had to be entirely her decision. Given their professional association—no matter how much of a technicality it was at this point—he refused to push and risk making her uncomfortable.

He was about to tell her that he'd just have the car take her home, but then she stepped forward and edged past him. He gripped her forearm before she continued, trapping both of them in the doorway so her breasts grazed his chest, and the scent of cinnamon filled his senses.

He started to ask if she was sure but shut his mouth fast. April Porter was more than capable of taking care of herself and making her own decisions. She was no wilting flower or insecure flirt. That was one of the hundred things he was coming to appreciate about her, and he wouldn't insult her intelligence by suggesting she didn't know her own mind.

She looked up at him, her hesitation gone. The only thing left glistening in her gaze was a combination of expectation and promise.

He kissed her. Hard. Hot. Blatantly telling her how pleased he was with her decision. They moved out of the entryway, and he tipped the door closed with his foot without releasing her.

She tore her mouth from his and looked over his shoulder. "Lock it," she ordered.

"Always looking out for me?"

Fielding was in custody. The threat had been neutralized, and there was nothing to worry about anymore, but he reached back and did it anyway because otherwise he knew she wouldn't be able to lose herself in the moment and enjoy all the things he was going to do to her.

"It's my job," she said, "and as long as I'm getting paid — "

Her gaze widened in horror, and she drew back sharply. He flinched and grabbed her hand, refusing to let her retreat. "Don't," he said firmly. "The job is finished. This is just between us."

"That might be true if we hadn't started this long before the job was done."

"It doesn't matter. Everything worked out," he reassured her. "All that matters now…is now."

"One night for pleasure," she said, biting her lip. "Let's have this one night to give in to it, to be reckless and wild with one another."

One night? They were free, and all she wanted was one night? That was usually more than enough for him, but with her…he didn't want to think about being done with her. Not yet. "April — "

"One night, Nolan," she repeated firmly. "After tonight, I'll be moving on to another assignment and helping my dad get through his treatment. You'll be taking the business world by storm and going to more of those fancy business parties. We're not even going to exist in the same stratosphere. We both know that beyond tonight, it would never work between us."

"I haven't gotten where I am today by refusing a challenge."

"Are you saying that you want a relationship? The messy kind with lots of strings and expectations and compromise?" Her beautiful lips pursed. Was she asking him, or making it a proposal?

His grip on her hand tightened, but he hesitated.

Her chin tipped, but then she smiled and leaned in to kiss him. "One night," she murmured in a low voice, between breaths. "But I have no doubt you'll make it a night to remember."

"For the rest of your life," he murmured. He worked his hands into her hair until he heard pins dropping to the wood floor, dragged her full against him, and kissed her with all the urgency that was racing through his veins.

Her body was hot right through the slinky, thin fabric of her dress. She was a marvel of toned muscle and lush curves, and he wanted to immortalize every line, from the top to the bottom. She moaned into his mouth and gave him her tongue, and the taste of her defied all reason, made him weak in the knees. He backed her up against the wall, mostly to keep his legs from collapsing beneath him.

He took her face in his hands. Her eyes were already bright with rising desire. Her breaths were short and quick. "*Goddamn*," he muttered with a sweeping wave of awe and euphoria. A man could get high just watching her. And *he'd* put that look on her face.

Clothes. Too many freaking clothes.

He felt for the zipper of her dress up by her shoulder blades and dragged it down the length of her spine, trying to go slowly and savor every moment of the reveal, but he felt clumsy and desperate.

The zipper stopped just at the top of her ass where it started to flare out, and he slipped both hands inside. Her skin was so soft, irresistible to the touch. So he touched. And touched. His hands smoothed up and down her back and cupped her sumptuous ass. She squirmed against him and it felt so good he wanted to lift her leg up around his hip and drive his cock in her right there.

He pulled the dress apart, intending to drag the straps from her shoulders, but froze at the sound of fabric ripping. "Shit."

She chuckled. "There's a hook at the neckline, in addition to the zipper," she said. She turned around and pulled her long hair over her shoulder, glancing back at him with a molten, sultry expression that only increased his desperation.

"I'll have it fixed for you, and it'll be good as—"

"Just get it off me. Hurry." Her voice broke. He flipped open the fastening of her dress. It spread apart, a deep V down the beautiful slope of her back. "You inspire me," he said. He wrapped his forearm around her waist and pulled her into the cradle of his body. He peppered kisses all the way down her spine, bending her over until she braced a hand against the wall. "I want to write poetry all over your body. With chocolate. And then lick it off."

"I didn't know you wrote poetry." Her voice was already guttural and broken, which made him smile.

"I don't."

"How else do I inspire you?" she asked. Her ass pressed back into his hips.

"Let me count the ways," he said, grinding the thick bulge of his aching cock against her.

With a gasp, she straightened and spun to face him. He took a few steps back to take it all in. Her eyes glimmered.

Her face flushed. Her chest rose and fell beneath the gaping fabric of her dress.

He was spellbound. She was the most magnificent thing he'd ever seen…and he would have her tonight.

Chapter Eleven

They were seriously beyond the point of no return. Even if she hadn't been able to see it in his eyes, she felt it in her bones and coursing through her veins.

Was she absolutely sure about this? She was crossing more and more professional lines every second here. Shouldn't she be more concerned about that?

She wasn't. Maybe she'd still been a little uncertain about making assumptions when Nolan picked her up earlier, but not anymore. Any guilt about letting her professional and personal lives mix was gone.

She gazed at Nolan and hunched her shoulders, letting her dress fall. It slithered down her body to the floor, leaving her standing before him in nothing but her bra and thong... and her garter, which hadn't been holding up her stockings ever since the car and she was lucky they hadn't sagged down to her ankles by now.

He watched her with such intensity that her skin burned, but then she watched him, too. He shrugged off his jacket, tugged at his expertly knotted tie until it loosened, and started to undo the buttons of his shirt. She shivered with anticipation. With need.

They both kicked off their shoes at the same time, and then Nolan came after her again, sweeping her up in his arms. As one, they stumbled across the living room through the doors to the darkened bedroom.

He flipped on a small table lamp by the bed and she paused.

His brow lifted. "I want to be able to see every inch of you, all night long," he said.

Boxing and training had kept her in good shape, and there'd always been guys around the gym to feed her ego if she'd wanted that. But her dad had always discouraged those relationships. The only guys who'd made a serious play for her had been the kind who'd been out to prove something. To her, to her father, to the world. In the ring, those guys went after one thing, and out of it, they'd looked for a different sort of prize. But she'd known better, and she'd been focused on her own goals. None of those boys had ever seriously tempted her. No one had ever *seriously* tempted her.

Except for one, and that had turned out...badly.

She crawled up onto the brand new mattress that had been covered with fresh sheets and a luxurious duvet, and motioned for him to join her there. It dipped with his weight as he obliged and immediately reached for her. She eased back across the width of the wide bed, with him on top.

Ah geez, he covered her like a big electric blanket, hot and heavy. It was the best feeling in the world...or so she thought for as long as it took for him to start kissing her again, and then so many new bests hit her one after the other it became impossible to rate them.

He removed her bra and panties and worshipped her breasts with his mouth, and—Jesus. His hands. His hands moved over her skin with both precision and urgency, raising goose bumps like a map to tell her where he'd been and where he still had to go. Everywhere. He went everywhere, playing her like a harp. A shivering, moaning, orgasming harp.

She was still shuddering with aftershocks when he reached into the dresser drawer and pulled on a condom, but he braced himself above her and entered her so slowly, making sure she felt every amazing inch of him sinking deep as he looked down into her eyes.

When he paused, she wrapped her legs around his waist. He reached between them to tweak her clit, and when he started to draw back she dug her fingernails into the tensed muscles of his biceps. Three long strokes, and she was going off all over again.

"Oh my God, Steve." She gasped. She'd never directly addressed him by his first name before this moment, but if there was ever a time to dispense with formality, it should be now, right?

She opened her mouth over the thick muscle of his shoulder and bit down in an attempt to stem the flood of overwhelming sensation and complicating emotion.

"Ah fuck." His whole body went beautifully rigid for several long moments, and then released.

Afterward, he held her close, dropping his head into the cradle of her neck. She felt him struggling to control his breathing, like her. She tasted the saltiness of his sweat-dampened skin, and saw the sheen on her own. She felt his heart hammering wildly, creating a musical beat in time with hers as their chests pressed together.

Here in the dark they were in perfect sync for a single brief moment, as if both of their very different worlds had stopped spinning just long enough to torture her with how perfect it could be between them. It was almost enough for her to believe that tomorrow morning would never come, and they wouldn't have to get up to face different paths when the sun came through the big windows.

She closed her eyes. It was a lie, but she could pretend. Morning wouldn't arrive for a few more hours.

Chapter Twelve

It was still early in the morning, although the sun had indeed risen and nothing would keep the day away. April slipped out from Nolan's forearm and got up to give her teeth a finger brushing in the adjoining bathroom. She snagged his dress shirt from last night on the way and pulled it on.

When she was done, she returned to Nolan's room but stopped halfway to the bed. She looked down at him, stretched out like a beautiful warrior prince waiting for his harem to come tend to him, and gulped as her imagination went crazy.

They'd made a deal for one night only, and the night was definitely over. She should probably turn around and get a move on. It would be smarter if she were already dressed before he awakened. The two of them would be less likely to submit to temptation again.

But she couldn't look away. And then he stirred, and she was irresistibly drawn closer. One last time before they let the world back in? He had driven her over the edge so often last night but never let her take control, and she wanted a turn.

Slowly climbing back on the bed, she lifted the hem of

the shirt she still wore and settled over his thighs, biting her lip at the naughty feel of her bare pussy pressed to his skin. She thought he must be awake and would open his eyes then, but he didn't. Boldly, she spread her palms over his pecs and retraced the hills and valleys of the muscular figure she'd gotten to know so well last night, all the way to his hips.

His cock was filling out, growing hard. She touched a single finger to the tip and smiled when it jerked toward her. Oh yes, he was awake. And he deserved to be teased within an inch of his life.

"Are you going to join me?" she asked huskily and cupped her breasts. "Or am I just playing with myself here?"

He groaned and snapped his gaze open. She crossed her arms and pulled the shirt over her head and shook her hair back out of her face.

"Damn, you are without a doubt the most amazing thing I've ever woken up to," he muttered in a voice hoarse with sleep and desire, while his eyes glittered with electric energy. He put his hands on her knees and slipped them up her thighs in silent but unmistakable encouragement for her to come closer. "I didn't want to open my eyes, in case it was all just an overactive wet dream."

She wasn't ready to let him call the shots. She pinched her nipples and bit her lip at the stab of delicious pleasure-pain. "And do you have those often?"

"I have a feeling I'll be having them a lot more, now that I know exactly what to dream about." He put his hands on her hips and tried shifting her forward, but she shook her head. She wasn't finished torturing him just yet.

She slipped her hands down her belly to the triangle between her spread legs and dipped one finger into her own slick heat while he looked up at her with eager intensity.

She circled her clit and shuddered as gentle waves shot through her.

"Go deeper," he murmured, his grip on her hips tightening. He dragged her forward so she wasn't sitting on his thighs anymore but right on top of his erection.

"Hey, I'm the one in control here," she replied, but she lifted just enough to slide her middle finger deep.

"Two fingers," he said. "Do it."

She didn't bother to argue with his bossiness this time. Two fingers. She was fucking herself with two fingers right in front of Steve Nolan, his hard cock an insistent presence under the crack of her ass.

He bucked beneath her, and she threw her head back and closed her eyes, giving in to the pounding of her heart and the throbbing pressure building in her core. She was so close. God, so close. But this wasn't what she'd planned, so with a final stroke and a deep breath, she eased back again and wrapped her wet fingers around his penis.

She swiped her thumb over the head before leaning over him and licking up the drop of moisture that appeared there. His back bowed as she took more of him in, but before she could settle in to drive him right over the edge, he flipped her over and knelt between her legs.

She looked up. "I wasn't finished!" she cried.

"Oh, we're not finished," he assured her with a wicked smile. "Not by a long shot."

She knew exactly where he was going when his head dipped down, and she shook with anticipation. His hands were a firm weight on her inner thighs, pushing her legs wider.

She bucked almost completely off the bed when his tongue licked all the way up her pussy like a cherry Popsicle. Nolan shifted so he was flat on his stomach. He cupped her ass cheeks and held her right up to his face. She could only see his eyes, and they looked all the way up her body right into her face and held there.

His tongue pierced her again and again, while keeping

her orgasm maddeningly out of reach. But finally he lifted his head and reached into the drawer for a condom. She lifted her arms to take him, but he shook his head and guided her onto her stomach.

He'd seized control from her just like that, and he tormented her for a long, erotic hour. But as she lay by herself in the middle of the bed afterward, trying to regulate her breathing and savoring aches in places she hadn't ever felt before, somehow she didn't mind having given in once again. She couldn't keep the smile off her face.

The shower came on in the bathroom. That meant the new day had indeed come. April stretched and her stomach growled. She got up and looked around for Nolan's shirt again. It had ended up crumpled at the foot of the bed. She grabbed it and padded out to the kitchen before remembering that there hadn't been much to eat the last time she was there.

She opened the refrigerator door. It was full. There were eggs, milk, juice, fruit, and vegetables. All normal things one expected to find in a refrigerator.

"The maid brought a few things for me after the insurance crew was done in here."

Of course he had a maid to do groceries for him. Only regular people went out to buy their own food. Yep, reality was definitely poking its ugly face into her glow.

She looked up to see him standing there, wearing nothing but a towel around his waist. His skin gleamed, and his damp hair stuck straight up on top of his head like he'd just rubbed the towel through it a couple of times.

"You look good in my shirt." He was looking her up and down like he would rather eat her for breakfast than anything she could put on the stove. "Your legs go on for miles, and I'm already devising reasons to make you bend over and show me more."

Self-conscious, she tugged, but the hem already hit her

almost to the knee. If she turned and bent over, he wasn't getting that good a look at her ass.

He shook his head with a grin. "Not the back," he said, gazing pointedly at her gaping neckline. She hadn't done up all the buttons, and if she bent even just a tiny bit, he would have a perfect view of absolutely everything.

Nolan crowded her into the open refrigerator and nuzzled her neck. The cold made her nipples poke through the white fabric of the dress shirt. "Let's stay here today and forget about everything else," he murmured.

The urge to say yes was almost crippling, but if she agreed, how hard would it be to leave tomorrow?

Maybe he won't want you to leave then, either.

No, maybe not tomorrow, or even the next day. But one day he would be telling his friends that it was time to get serious. Guys like him fucked girls like her, but they didn't get serious about girls like her. They got serious with girls who looked natural in an evening gown on a Wednesday night and went to the country club after hosting a dinner party the night before, while their kids scavenged the pantry for gourmet crackers.

Someone had to leave; that's the way it worked. She'd rather it be her, and she'd rather it be now, while she still had a chance of doing it without losing another piece of her soul to the pain of loss.

"You wanted to get answers from Edward Fielding," she reminded him with a sigh. "And I'll probably have a new assignment waiting for me."

"What if I've decided that I like having a bodyguard?" He traced a finger across her collarbone and dipped into the neckline of her shirt. "Maybe I'll just keep you."

"Don't." She stiffened. "I've already screwed up my chances in one career and what happened last night was *this* close to crossing the boundaries of the only respectable job prospect that I have left open to me."

"Are you saying you regret what we did?"

"I have no regrets, but I won't pretend it was anything more or less than—"

"What?" His jaw clenched. "What do you think this was?"

She sighed. "You know. It's no secret. We're from different worlds, Nolan. We have different paths. You're on the verge of becoming a household name, and I…" She paused.

"You're…?"

"A convenient way to keep your mind off everything."

He dropped his arm. "So, let me get this straight. You're nothing but my convenient distraction so that I won't have to deal with being targeted by a psychopath." She wouldn't nod, but she didn't deny it. He stepped back, his expression blank. "And I suppose I'm your distraction, too, aren't I?"

His words hit her like a slap to the face, even though he hadn't said as much as he could have. He hadn't said that she was using him to stem her fear for her father, for example. Or using him to forget her failures for a little while. And yet, the way he looked at her, he was really saying all those things and more.

Her hand fluttered at her throat.

He waited. Waited for her to say something. *What?* What was she supposed to say?

All the words choking her felt so…vulnerable. If she said them, gave him what he seemed to want, and he took her back into his arms, into his bed…into his *life*, how long before she loved him completely?

Based on her feelings now? Not long.

She stepped up to slip past him, her shoulder and the side curve of her breast brushing his arm.

The electricity was immediate. She made the mistake of looking up at him instead of starting out of the room like she should and went completely still. He drew in a sharp breath, and his gaze flared with heat. Could he see it in her eyes? How much she still wanted him? How badly she was failing at denying it?

"April," he whispered.

She curled her fingers over his shoulders and pulled him closer just as he buried his hand in her hair and tugged her head back. He crushed his mouth to hers without any finesse, but it was exactly what she wanted. It wasn't the slick, polished Steve Nolan in his business suit that made her hot. She wanted this raw, real Steve Nolan. The one who put on boxing gloves and wasn't afraid to sweat, and ate cookies on the kitchen floor, and made her feel like an Amazon.

And the knowledge that she couldn't really have him only made the want sharper.

She kissed him back with every bit of the frustration, anger, and disappointment that she'd felt ever since waking up this morning.

They were as desperate to touch one another as they'd been in the beginning, as they'd been all night long.

Wrong. Wrong. Wrong. She was supposed to let go today. The morning had come, and with it, revelations that made it even smarter for her to keep her distance. And yet here she was, reveling in the feel of his tongue slipping into her mouth, the feel of his arms holding her so tightly she almost felt... cherished.

She pushed against his chest with a gasp. "Steve...Nolan, I can't." The taste of him was still heavy on her mouth, and the words stuck thick in her throat, but she squared her shoulders. "Our night is over," she reminded him.

He grinned and reached for her. "What's the point of making rules, if you don't get to break them?"

She jerked back and shook her head. "Not this time," she whispered. "It's too complicated."

He saw the hesitation in her eyes. He saw the tremor in

her arms. Her nipples were still so tight with need they were hard points through the cotton of his shirt. She wanted him so badly, she was shaking from it even as she moved to go.

"It doesn't have to be complicated," he said. "We could have some fun together. Who knows what might happ—"

"I know what will happen, and I can't do it," she interrupted. She had to get out now or she'd give in to his unspoken promise and sign on the dotted line, knowing full well that he'd be lying to himself and her.

She bit her lip. It could be worth it.

What are you doing? Her heart sputtered, froze. She couldn't. Couldn't do it. Couldn't give him what he wanted. Couldn't let…

His frown deepened with disappointment as the silence stretched across the ocean suddenly between them.

"You don't want anything more than this," she murmured. He didn't. He couldn't.

"You're so sure about that?" He paused for a long moment, but then he shrugged as if all this talk had only been hypothetical. "Well, I guess you're right. Why ruin something fun with a lot of seriousness? It's not my style, anyway."

"Bad for the colon," she whispered. Her own smile wouldn't quite come.

"Exactly." He kissed her. Light. No pressure, no urgency, no expectations.

She let out a fractured sigh and tried to ignore the heavy ball of lead in the hollow pit of her stomach. "You're cold," she choked out.

"We *are* standing inside my refrigerator, and I *am* pretty close to naked," he murmured.

How she could have forgotten with all that male flesh staring her in the face… "Oh! I was going to make some eggs," she said.

A loud buzzing startled them both just as she turned to

get the eggs and let the fridge door close. "The door." He started for the front door.

She followed and stopped him before he could open it. "Don't answer it. Let me check first."

"I'm not your assignment anymore, remember?" He gave her that look, but she pointed to the towel barely clinging to his waist with a grin. He crossed his arms and propped his shoulder against the kitchen entrance.

She couldn't figure out why he was grinning back at her until he raised an eyebrow at *her* attire. She stretched onto her toes and squinted through the keyhole, but when she saw who was on the other side, she spun around and put her back to the door, eyes wide.

"Who is it?" Nolan asked, arms crossed over a chest that could distract her, even now.

"It's your *mother*." She clenched her eyes shut and shook her head. Pants. Where were her damn pants? "And I *don't* need to meet her for only the second time ever…like *this*."

"Steven? Open up, please," Mrs. Nolan said through the door.

April opened her eyes and Nolan was coming out of the bedroom, having tugged on a pair of warmup pants but still no shirt. Why did he have pants but hers were gone? What kind of fucked-up karma was that?

"I have no pants!" she hissed, running into the bedroom. Just the dress she'd been wearing last night, and that wasn't exactly the message of professionalism she wanted to present to the mother of the man she was supposed to be protecting with her life. "Don't you dare open that door."

He glanced through the peephole and chuckled. "She's not going to go away, you know. Doug will have told her I'm up here."

"Then you had better help me find something to wear."

"Steven, it's your mother. Are you going to let me in?"

April groaned, wishing she could melt right through the floor as she swung the door almost all the way closed and hid behind it like a guilty teenager.

Nolan opened the door. "Hey Mother, what are you doing here?" she heard him ask. She peeked through the crack and watched the slim woman stepping forward to embrace him. He pressed an affectionate kiss on her cheek.

"You didn't return my calls last night. And after that nasty business with Justin Fielding's son and all the awful things they're saying in the news, I needed to see you, to make sure you were all right." She touched his cheek reverently, and April's heart lurched with a sudden memory of her own mother doing almost exactly the same.

"I'm fine, but a bit busy right now," he said. "I want to tell you everything, but can it wait for a little later?"

Mrs. Nolan took in her son's state of undress and looked around the apartment with pursed lips. April swore under her breath as the woman stopped and saw the pair of heels April had kicked off last night. They were still in the middle of the living room. Her small clutch purse was draped over the chair.

Mrs. Nolan raised her brows with obvious distaste. "The bodyguard?"

April winced and inched backward but tripped over the towel Nolan must have discarded on the floor when he'd grabbed his pants. She landed on her butt and didn't hear Nolan's response, but as she sat there with her eyes closed and her back up against the wall beside the door, she heard everything else.

"Do you think that's wise?"

"Since when do you care what I do with my personal life?" he replied.

"Personal life? If I understand correctly, she was working for you."

"I wouldn't quite put it like that," he said.

"And I've always cared. I want nothing but the best for you, and that woman is *not* it." April gasped. She could understand why Nolan's mother would not approve, but to put it like that was going a bit far. "I suppose you don't know that she's already told all the newspapers that she's sleeping with you?"

What?

"I seriously doubt that, Mother," Nolan said impatiently. "She would never have told anybody anything."

"Then why did someone from the country club send me a link this morning to an online article in which someone named April Porter is quoted as calling you 'the best money she ever made'? The same article printed a tawdry photograph of the two of you all over each other in the elevator of this very apartment building."

April groaned. This couldn't be happening. The photo had to be a fake—wait, the night they'd come up to find Nolan's apartment trashed and he'd kissed her…when the elevator door had opened, she'd sworn she saw something. But she'd been distracted. Hadn't been doing her job. This was her fault.

His mother was mid-sentence, "…besides, I thought you were seeing Jennifer Halloway. When I talked to her at the gala yesterday evening, she mentioned that she'd had dinner with you just a few nights ago."

April put a hand over her eyes. Distracted again. Had she been so absorbed by her dance with Nolan last night that she hadn't even seen the tall, red-haired bombshell at the party? "We did have dinner a few times, but it was never serious between us."

She let out a sigh. She'd believed him when he told her the same thing. She shouldn't have cared, though. After this morning, she had even less of a right to be concerned with Nolan's casual affairs—past, present, or future. She'd practically insisted on being nothing more than one of them.

"Frankly, that's probably a good thing. She's not the right woman for you, either," his mother said. "But I worry about you. It's one thing to let off a little steam and have some fun, but your business is taking off, and you could use a real partner at your side."

"I have a partner for my business, Mother. I think Harrison would be offended to hear that you don't consider his contributions worthy."

"You know that isn't what I mean. Why do you always have to be a smart aleck?"

April sympathized wholeheartedly.

"Spit it out," he said. "What are you getting at?"

"I'm saying that it's time to get serious and make some serious plans for the rest of your life." April's heart lurched at the word "serious."

"Maybe that's what I'm doing," he said, making April's mouth fall open until she remembered that he was the king of antagonism and provocation.

"Oh, please. You don't get serious with the *bodyguard*," she said dismissively, and April winced. "I've always thought that you and Meredith would be a wonderful match."

"Mother—"

April remembered the smile on his face when he'd been speaking to Meredith on his cell phone. *Who he'd also said was just a friend.*

"Meredith is beautiful, successful, and she comes from a good family—one of the only families that stood by us during the horrible period after your father's death," she said. "And you've always loved her, at least."

"Yes, but—"

April pressed a hand over her mouth and scrambled up off the floor. *You've always loved her.* She couldn't stop hearing the words in her head. She grabbed her dress and rushed to the bathroom and closed the door, shutting out anything else

Nolan and his mother might be saying about the beautiful, perfect love of Nolan's life.

She stood under the steaming water in the shower, berating herself for her reaction. Why would it bother her if Nolan had feelings for another woman? Hadn't she been the one to insist—just like a spooked chicken—that there was no chance of anything between them beyond last night? That it was all just fun and games, and they would each go back to their separate lives once this assignment was all wrapped up?

So why did the knowledge that Nolan's mother didn't find her worthy of her son hurt so much? Why did her heart ache to hear that he was in love with someone else?

Someone knocked on the door. Nolan. She didn't answer and stayed exactly where she was until the water ran cold.

Chapter Thirteen

April had taken her time getting ready. Plenty of time. Her dress was a little wrinkled, but it would get her home. She'd towel-dried her hair and pulled it all back into a damp bun. Then she called the hospital and had another painful conversation with her father. He told her to stop fussing and stay away, and she swallowed her disappointment and frustration because she didn't want to add to his pain.

Finally, she called Nora, who tactfully refrained from asking how her night went and didn't mention the article on the internet. She *did* confirm that the rest of the guard detail had been pulled off of Nolan's apartment last night, although they'd left one guy over at Mrs. Nolan's house until morning. Nora also advised that the police would allow Nolan to speak with Edward Fielding this morning…apparently at Fielding's insistence. In fact, he'd refused to speak with anyone *but* Nolan.

When she returned to the kitchen, Nolan's mother had left, and *he* was making eggs. She bit her lip and tugged at the hem of her skirt. He dished out the contents of the frying pan into two plates and brought them to the table.

"Steve, I…I heard a little of your conversation with Mrs. Nolan. I'm so sorry about that photograph. It never should have ended up online."

He frowned up at her. "Did you *know* about it?"

She winced at the hard edge in his voice. "Well, I—"

"So it's true."

He was buying everything his mother had said—that she wasn't up to his level, that she would stoop to selling him out to the tabloids.

Not even bothering to defend herself, she nodded. "Yes, it's my fault." Which was true. Because of her distraction, she'd been responsible for yet another torrid story about him showing up in the papers. She'd been responsible for the attack on him at the gala. She was so far from professional, it was laughable.

He dropped both plates to the table with a clatter. One of them loudly rocked all the way around on its rim before coming to a stop. "Enjoy your breakfast. I'm going to get dressed."

She looked at the eggs, but couldn't eat a thing.

Yes, their one night was definitely over now.

He refused to wait for her to get a taxi home so she could change and then come back for him before going to the police station. "Not my bodyguard anymore, remember? You don't have to come with me," he said.

She crossed her arms. "I'd like to see it through to the end." She refused to acknowledge that she was looking for excuses to get more time with him.

"I don't need you there," he insisted sharply.

His coldness hurt. Where had she heard that before? She

clenched her jaw and nodded. "All right, if that's what you want. But if you do need something, just—"

"I won't."

She left the apartment, but stood outside in the hallway in front of the elevator, frowning. She couldn't just leave it like that.

When she spun back around to knock on his door, he'd already opened it again. He was still pulling on his jacket as he pulled the door closed behind him when he glanced up and saw her. "You're still here."

She stepped forward. "Nolan, I just want to say—"

"I've got to get to the police station." He tugged the sleeves of his suit and adjusted the collar of his shirt as he moved past her to the stairwell and pushed open the door.

She followed. "I'm sorry," she said again. "When the elevator door opened that night, I swore I heard something— the click of the camera I suppose. I should have checked it out. I shouldn't have let them get away with—"

He stopped and turned to glare down at her. "I don't care about the damn photograph," he snapped. "The fucking article *quoted* you. You talked to them."

Her mouth dropped open. "You think that I..." She shook her head quickly. "Nolan, that quote was bullshit. Yes, I should have been better at my job and prevented the photograph, but I never spoke to a reporter. They made that up completely, I promise."

"How much did they pay you?"

She took a step back. "You think that I would take money for..."

He swore and ran a hand through his hair. "It wouldn't be the first time."

She sneered. "I might be a horrible bodyguard, and a poor nobody from the wrong side of the tracks who ate dinners out of a vending machine as a kid, but that doesn't automatically mean I'd sell you out."

She reached for the door.

"April, I didn't mean—"

He reached for her arm. She jerked it back.

A sound on the stairwell broke through their argument. It was like a gurgle of pain, and a choked scream of fury all at the same time. April looked up with a gasp, and as soon as she saw who stood in the stairwell watching them, a few steps down, she knew she'd made a horrible mistake.

It was the woman from the elevator in Nolan's office, the woman from the restaurant. She'd slipped into the stairwell, and April had a good feeling that it wasn't the first time. Whatever Edward Fielding had wanted from Nolan last night, he wasn't the one who'd broken in and trashed his apartment, and he wasn't the one who'd slashed Nolan's tires.

The look on her face was twisted with such naked rage as she raised her arm...and pointed a gun straight at them.

Oh shit. "Miss," she said slowly, like talking to a jumper on the ledge. "Miss, you don't want to do anything—"

"April, be careful," Nolan said in warning, taking her hand tightly.

The woman's face crumpled when he said *her* name. April's. Almost as if she'd thought he would see her and be overcome with...what? Love? Regret? April winced and immediately put herself in front of Nolan.

"*April?*" she sneered. She shook the gun at them, making April more nervous. "I've loved you all this time, and you say another woman's name to my face?"

"Veronica?" Nolan's gaze shifted from the gun to the woman. He took a careful step forward. "It was one night, a long time ago. I never meant to hurt you. I'm very sorry if you thought—"

"One night wasn't enough," she said with a hitch in her voice. "If you'd only given me a chance, you would have seen.

We could have had—"

"You're absolutely right," Nolan quickly agreed. "If you put the gun down, we can start over. We can have dinner or something, and—"

The woman's arm wavered and April tensed. "How can I believe you?" she screamed, shaking the gun at April. "When I come up here and see you with *her*!"

It happened so fast. April knew the gun was going to go off. She lunged forward to protect Nolan, but he shoved her aside.

The bang reverberated in the stairwell. Nolan shouted and was thrown back against the wall. As he slid down, he left a streak of red on the concrete. "Steve!" she cried out.

Veronica was already swinging the gun her way, but April tackled her. The gun flew out of Veronica's hand as the two of them rolled down the stairs together.

April grunted as the step jammed her in the ribs and again when she bashed her temple on the wall, and when she and Veronica stopped rolling, the woman jumped on her and backhanded her across the mouth.

April was winded. She tasted blood on her lip but ignored it. She was used to taking a hit.

She swung a punch—no wimpy slaps—and Veronica's head cracked back, and April pushed her off her.

The woman screamed and jumped to her feet. "Back off!" Nolan stood over them with the gun trained on Veronica, his other hand pressed to the bleeding wound in his side.

She quickly raised both hands in surrender but turned a sneer toward April. "If you think he's going to stay with you just because you had his attention for one night, you're deluding yourself," she spat, blood dripping from her nose. "He's just a shallow rich boy, and he'll move on soon enough. He always does."

April ignored her and raced back up the steps for her

purse. Nolan kept the gun trained on Veronica as she dug out her cell phone and dialed 911.

Steve lay in a damn hospital bed. Apparently, he'd spent three hours on the operating table after the emergency room doc had declared that the bullet had chipped a rib on the way through his body, and they had to go in to check things out. They'd rolled up a gurney and made him get on it right then and there. The last thing he remembered seeing before finally giving in to the need to pass out was April's drawn, severe expression. She hadn't said a word to him since the ambulance had arrived at the apartment, and he'd wanted to tell her not to worry about anything, but all he'd gotten out was her name…and didn't remember anything else.

She hadn't returned since he regained consciousness here in the recovery room, and he was already going stir crazy lying around all by himself.

"That's it," he muttered, shoving aside the nurse's call button and the tube across his arm, and struggling to sit up. His body protested the movement vociferously, sending pain shooting in all directions from the relative nucleus of the bandaged hole in his side. But he wasn't giving up. He needed to find April.

The door opened just as he swung his legs over the mattress with a deep grunt. "I don't think you're supposed to be up yet," Harrison said from the entrance.

"Are you just going to stand there, or are you going to help me?"

His friend came forward and took Nolan's arm…then guided him back down into the bed. "That's not helping," Steve muttered.

"Says you."

Harrison undid the button of his jacket and sat down in the chair beside the bed. He settled in like he had all the time in the world. "Why are you here?" Steve was getting grumpier by the minute.

"Your bodyguard called me while you were in surgery."

His heart leaped. Where was she? "I'm fine," Steve said. "I just want to get out of here."

Harrison chuckled. "I have it on good authority that you're going to be stuck in this room for at least one full night."

"Where's April?"

Harrison's brow lifted knowingly, as if he'd been waiting to see how long he'd hold out before asking. "She's been standing guard outside your room since you came out of surgery."

Why didn't she come in? Despite the arc of agony through his abdomen, Steve shifted to get out of bed again, but Harrison stood and stopped him. "I'll bring her in, but Jesus, don't pop a stitch and start bleeding. I have no desire to suffer that woman's wrath."

Steve frowned. "What do you mean?"

He chuckled. "She's been very protective of you. The cops have tried to get in here to ask you a bunch of questions, but after she was done setting them straight, they left looking like first-year rookies who'd been reamed out by their commanding officer—without her even raising her voice or lifting a finger."

Harrison went to the door and lowered his voice. "You know, we could probably use someone like her to run our security team. Nobody would *dare* steal corporate secrets with her around."

Steve shook his head. "She's destined for much bigger things," he said, grinning with pride. He didn't know if they were destined to go there together—he just knew he wanted to see her. Now. "Get her in here, would you? And then go away for a really long time."

Harrison looked amused and left the room, but the door didn't open again immediately. Was she really going to stay out there, avoiding him?

"Ms. Porter!" he shouted and then groaned. That hurt. But it got a reaction. The door swung open, and April stalked in. She was still wearing her dress from last night. It was wrinkled and dirty, and the bun in her hair was letting locks of her hair free to frame her face. She had a wicked black eye and another bruise tracing her jawline. But the dark smudge on her arm was blood. Dried blood. *His blood.*

Her gaze swept the room as if to confirm everything was still safe, carefully avoiding him directly until the very last possible moment. But when she locked on, there was fire in her eyes. Even with the pain meds and who knew what else flowing through his bloodstream, he was suddenly hard beneath the thin hospital gown.

"Do you require assistance, Mr. Nolan?" she asked coolly, crossing her arms. "I can fetch the doctor if you're unable to use the call button."

So it was going to be like that, was it?

"The only thing I need is you," he said bluntly, but her only reaction was a tightening around her mouth. "Are you okay?"

She nodded. "If that's all you wanted, I'll get your doctor to look you over, so that I can tell the police officers who've been waiting that they can come in to ask you some questions."

He swore. "Damn it, April. Get over here. We need to talk."

She tensed even more, like a pillar of stone that was hard and strong but would explode into a billion pieces if someone came along and pushed it over.

He shrugged. "All right, if you aren't going to come over

here, then I'll have to get up and go to you." He started to swing his legs over the bed again, not even having to pretend the gasp of discomfort that blew from his mouth.

She rushed over. "Oh! Get back in bed, you jerk. You're the most disobedient, stubborn, practically certifiable—"

He let his head fall back into the pillow with a groan. It was a good thing that had worked because standing on his own might actually have been a problem. "I knew you'd give in. You'd never let anyone hurt me, not even myself."

She snorted and put her hands on her hips. "Only because I haven't been paid yet."

He didn't believe her. Not after last night. Not after this morning. She couldn't kiss him like she did and not feel about him the way he felt about her. He remembered the hurt in her eyes when he'd turned cold and accused her of selling him out to the rags. He remembered the devastation on her face when that bullet had ripped into him.

And he remembered the way he'd felt when she went tumbling head over heels down the steps, wrestling for the gun with Veronica.

Screw expectations. Screw what was good for business. Screw his past. Screw the complications.

The future was what mattered...and he no longer had any doubt that April Porter was his future.

"What did you want to talk about?" she asked, wary.

With that settled, he assessed the situation like he would assess any business plan or mathematical problem. Which sequence was going to ensure the result he was looking for?

"I assume the police have Veronica in custody?" he started slow, easy.

Her lips pursed. "Yes, but we all know what happened the last time I assumed you were safe."

He knew where she was going with that and stopped her. "You couldn't have known the woman would be lying in wait in the stairwell of my building."

"Maybe. Maybe not." Her face twisted into an expression of disgust. "If I'd been less interested in getting laid and better at my job, maybe I'd have known about a great many other things, too, like the photograph of us in the elevator, and Edward Fielding at the—"

"Whoa." He wasn't going to let her blame herself. "I'm the one who arrogantly insisted that this whole thing was probably a harmless business tactic, that there was no way it was personally motivated. I said there couldn't possibly be a woman out there I'd hurt so horribly she'd be driven to violence over it. So let's not compare who was more wrong, because I'm pretty sure that I'm going to win."

A small smile pulled at her lips. "Okay, you've got me there."

"It's got to be a record, though, right?" he said. "Who else gets two stalkers at the very same time? Do we know which one of them wrote the notes, broke into my apartment, and slashed my tires?"

"Actually, Edward Fielding has an alibi for the night your apartment was broken into, and he says he didn't slash your tires, either, even though he is definitely the man I saw outside the clothing store that day."

"Why was he following me?"

She paused. "Apparently, he wanted to return the money that his father stole from your father ten years ago."

"He *what*?"

She nodded. "He told the police that he didn't know what his father had done—he'd only been sixteen at the time. He said he just remembered being forced to leave his home in the middle of the night and ending up in Colombia. His father did die in that car accident two years later. Edward apparently went away to school after that and only returned very recently to deal with his mother's estate when she passed away. In the course of this, he discovered a lock box in a bunch of his father's old things. It had some newspaper clippings and the key to a safety deposit box at the bank in Bogota. When he found the money there and put the facts together, he came to find you. He was outside your apartment that one morning the cameras got him on tape because he was hoping to talk to you, but you didn't come out. He said he followed you Saturday morning when we went shopping, but lost his nerve because you weren't alone."

"How did he know I was going to be at the gala last night?"

"Maybe he heard that your mother was the coordinator and simply decided that it was too difficult to get you alone, so he might have a better chance of talking to her."

"But why all the skulking around? If he really wanted to give back the money, there was no reason for him to be afraid."

"It's not *all* the money. It's whatever is left over after ten years. And don't forget, his father fled the country with the whole family. Fielding seems to have been worried that the police would determine they were all a part of it." She paused. "He wanted to do the right thing, but he didn't want to get in trouble. He slipped back into the U.S. without passing through an official border crossing."

Steve's side ached. He grimaced and shifted position with a bit of a groan. April immediately stepped forward and readjusted his pillow. He grasped her hand before she could jump away again.

"Why didn't you go home to change?" he asked. "You haven't washed. You look tired. Did the doctors check you out? When you fell down those stairs, I…"

She looked startled. Had no one else asked after her?

"I'm fine." She carefully pulled away from him and straightened. She looked down at herself and smoothed a hand over her hip, as if it was the first time her state of attire had registered. His fist clenched in the blanket. He hated that his blood stained her skin, that her hair had come loose. He wanted to draw her close. Wanted to hold her. Wanted to lay her back in a steaming bath and wash her from head to toe.

"I had a job to do," she said.

"Bullshit. Someone else could have done it."

She snorted and put her hands on her hips. "You were worried about me, admit it."

His head was starting to pound harder than before. His mouth was dry, and the ache in his side was a persistent stitch. "And you called *me* stubborn," he muttered when she still refused to give him what he wanted.

April frowned and touched his hand. "Nolan, do you need more pain meds?"

He grabbed on to her with all the energy he had left. "If I take them, do you promise you'll go get checked out?"

Her lips twitched. "Yes, boss."

He winced. "As of this moment, you don't work for me anymore."

Her gaze widened with hurt.

"Don't worry. You'll get paid for the job, but your duties are completed." He gritted his teeth against the increasing discomfort spreading through his body. "Which means you call me Steve, and you agree to go on a date with me when I get out of here."

She automatically stepped back and shook her head. "Nolan, I can't. It's more complicated than the employer/employee thing, and you know it."

"All I know is that we're good together. We're good in bed. We're good out of bed. We could be fucking *awesome*, but you live behind these walls that are so damn exhausting to scale."

"Maybe those walls are there for a reason," she whispered.

"I get it, believe me I do," he said, remembering how his father's blood splattered across the bedroom wall had looked exactly like the Rorschach blots the psychiatrists had made him look at for years afterward. "But one day, the walls will be so high and thick, that what you thought you'd created for your own protection will have become a prison."

"What are you, a shrink now?" she snapped defensively.

"I'm just a guy who's realized for the first time in his life that he wants something more," he admitted.

"There's no such thing, Nolan. Not between people like us. It's too hard."

"It doesn't have to be," he said, firm. He was making her a promise, if only she'd see it.

But she was already retreating. He could see it in her eyes even before her feet started to carry her back. She dropped the button for the self-administering meds drip on the mattress by his arm and was moving away from him faster than he could say morphine shot.

She paused before walking to the door. "I'll call Nora and make sure someone stands guard outside your room overnight," she murmured.

"Who hurt you? Who made you so afraid to take a chance?" He didn't know how he knew someone had, but she affirmed his suspicion when she flinched.

She clutched the doorframe, ready to propel herself through it.

"I never would have taken you for a coward, April Porter." The pain in his side exploded as his posture tightened with resolve. He'd made his case to her as best he could, but if she couldn't see it, if she couldn't let him in and trust in him—in *them*—he wouldn't beg.

He gave her a crisp nod as the ice settled in his chest. "Thank you for your professional assistance."

He ignored the hurt that broke across her face at his

abrupt and harsh dismissal. It wasn't enough. She wasn't prepared to give him more, and he couldn't settle for anything less. He went ahead and pressed the damn button. At least if the drugs knocked him out, he wouldn't have to lie there all night feeling sorry for himself.

Chapter Fourteen

April had no idea where she was going as she raced out of Nolan's room like the devil himself had lit a fire under her ass. All she knew was that if she had any chance of holding the line, of staying in control, she had to leave. Leave now and never look back.

A coward. That's exactly what she was.

She made it to the stairwell exit, but as she shoved open the door with a sob, she glanced up and saw the hospital directory posted on the wall.

5th Floor – Radiation

With a heavy heart, she went up instead of down. On the fifth floor, she hesitated before exiting the stairwell. But what else did she have to lose? She stopped at the main desk and waited for the pretty nurse in dark green scrubs to finish with her paperwork.

The nurse looked up, and the welcoming smile on her face froze as she took in April's appearance. "Are you okay?" she asked.

April glanced up and caught her reflection in the window

of the hospital room across the hall. She looked stunned, not to mention pale, bruised, and dirty. The rest of her—including the once beautiful dress she should never have bought—must look just as bad.

But inside, she felt...shattered. She was breaking apart into sharp pieces that cut and stabbed...and she wanted her father. "I'm looking for Mitchell Porter," April said weakly.

The nurse nodded and pointed back down the hall. "His room is four doors down that way." She flipped a few pages in her binder and said, "He's scheduled for a treatment in about twenty minutes."

"Thank you."

April found the room and lifted her fist. She stared at it hanging there in front of her for what seemed like forever before finally knocking.

"Yeah."

April's throat swelled at the thin, tired sound of her father's voice, and part of her wanted to turn and run.

Oh God. First Mom, and now Dad? Every time she walked into a hospital room, it felt like she was saying good-bye to someone.

And Nolan wanted to know why she refused to let her guard down? How was she supposed to love him, knowing it was just a matter of time before he left, too? He might not have to actually die to do it, but it was better to choose loneliness than to be blindsided with it after she'd gotten invested and comfortable.

She took a deep breath and pushed open the door. "Hey, Dad."

His head jerked up from the magazine in his lap. "April. What are you doing here?" His face lacked color, and his cheeks were gaunt. Even the breadth of his shoulders looked narrower. He wasn't the same man they'd called Mitch "the Ditch" back in the day because that's where he left all his opponents. He wasn't the same man who'd tossed her over his shoulders and made her screech with glee, and who'd taught her to throw a punch and keep her arms up to protect her face.

She took a few steps closer, restraining herself from running to him like she would have done any other day of her life. Not because she was afraid he would spurn her, but because she was afraid she'd start to cry...and then he would cry. She knew it right away. *That* was the real reason he hadn't wanted her to come. He'd known how hard this would be for her, and he hadn't wanted her to see him like this.

Her father squinted and looked her up and down. "What the hell happened to you?"

She choked out a laugh and cleared her throat. "I was attacked by a lunatic stalker in a stairwell."

He raised a brow. "In an evening dress?"

"Didn't you know? It's the latest fashion craze in bodyguard uniforms."

His mouth twitched. "Do I need to ask what the lunatic stalker looks like right now?"

"Worse, trust me," she said, gingerly touching her jaw. It hadn't ached so badly before. Then again, she'd been desperately trying to ignore pretty much everything...before.

Silence fell, and so did his smile. His shoulders drooped, and he opened his mouth.

"Don't," she whispered. "Don't make me go."

He sighed and patted the mattress. She swallowed hard and collapsed beside him in relief, crossing her knee under her. He put his arm around her and kissed her forehead. "I wish you had let me do it my way," he murmured. "I didn't want you to go through this." He took her hand and squeezed.

"I know. But you have to let me, and you have to trust that I can take it," she promised. Could she, though? She was so afraid of losing him, it was crippling. She was so afraid of losing *any* more people, she'd just *thrown away* the possibility of love. Her heart squeezed. "What I can't take is you shutting me out, because I love you too much."

"I know," he repeated in a soft voice. "I'll promise not to shut you out, if you promise not to shut out the world."

She frowned. "What makes you think I would—"

"Big Joey gave me a call," he said.

April groaned. "He was supposed to just get your answering machine," she grumbled.

"What's this about you and some highbrow client tossing sparks at one another on the mats?"

Her mouth dropped open. "Big Joey told you *that*?"

He chuckled. "You don't think he dialed up four different people to find out how to reach me just because you were looking good in a pair of gloves, do you?"

She groaned. "It was no big deal. Maybe I went a little easy on the guy, that's all."

"You don't go easy on anyone, ever. If they can't handle my girl at her best, they don't deserve you at any time." He chucked her in the arm. "So, does the suit deserve you?"

She sighed and stared out the window into the late afternoon sun. "It's…complicated, Dad. We have very different lives, and it's just…not a good time."

He tipped her face to look at him. "There's never a good time to fall in love. When I met your mother, I was hell-bent on becoming the next middleweight champion of the world. I wasn't thinking about romance and kids, but I saw her there at the train station, and everything changed just like that. She blew me off my feet."

Tears blurred her vision. "But if you hadn't married her, you wouldn't have had your heart broken when she died, and you wouldn't have had to give up on your dreams."

"Your mother became my only dream. And then you came along, and I realized that dreams were made to evolve and grow, like we all must evolve and grow."

He clutched her hand. His body might be frail, but his hands were still strong. Still big. Still capable. They were still her father's hands. "April, honey, you aren't going to make any dreams come true by locking your heart away out of reach."

Her breathing hitched with emotion. "But what if it all falls apart? It hurt so much to lose Mom, and then after Jeremy...I can't open up like that again."

"You're going to lose people. That's a part of life." They both knew it wasn't just Nolan they were talking about now, and April couldn't hold back the tears any longer. "And when it happens, you start over again, and you make new dreams with all the good memories from the old ones," he said.

"Dad."

"I want you to have every good thing that the world has to offer, and if this silver-spooned society boy"—she chuckled and shook her head—"makes you happy, then maybe that's where you should start."

She laughed but her world was spinning. "I would have to give him some boxing pointers," she teased. "He leads heavy."

A nurse came into the room. Her long red hair was peppered with silver, but she'd pulled it back into a fresh-looking ponytail that showed off flawless skin and bright green eyes. April discreetly wiped her cheeks and stood up from the bed.

"Hi, Dory." There was something in her father's voice as he greeted the nurse.

"Hey, Mitch." The woman's radiant smile could have lit up the room. April raised an eyebrow, and her father actually blushed. "Are you ready for your last treatment?" Dory asked.

"Um, can I come?" April said, hands twisting in front of her.

Her father nodded. "You and Dory can get acquainted. She's promised me we're goin' on a date when I get out of here," he said with a grin.

A couple of hours later, after helping her dad back to bed and getting him to drink a protein shake, April went back downstairs to Nolan's hospital room, but it was empty and the bed was already being turned down by a candy striper. *Too late.*

She went back out to the nurse's desk. "Did the patient in this room get moved?"

The nurse looked up with a frown. "Not exactly. He insisted on being released and left the hospital about an hour ago."

He'd left. Just like that.

April swore. She thanked the nurse and walked a few steps away for some privacy as she dug out her cell phone and called Nora. "Is Nolan still being covered?"

Her boss clucked. "Nope. That bankroll ship has sailed. He sent John home and said that after Edward Fielding and Ms. Ash, if someone else decided to stalk him anytime soon, he probably deserved it." She paused. "I've got another contract coming in as we speak, though. I can probably have you working in Manhattan again by tomorrow morning."

She sagged against the wall of the corridor. "Sorry Nora, but I'm going to need to take a leave of absence. I want to spend some time with my father and help him get back on his feet."

"I understand. Let me know if there's anything I can do to help, okay?"

She smiled weakly into her phone. "Thanks, but I think we just need some time to see if the radiation therapy worked and for him to get his strength back."

She hung up and checked for messages, but there were none. She tapped the screen to her contacts page, scrolling down until she found Nolan's number. Her thumb hesitated over the bubble that only had a shadow-figure inside it because she didn't have a photo to attribute to his profile.

Is that what these last few days were destined to be relegated to? A shadowy break from reality they were both going to forget had ever happened? Or could she make her dreams a reality with someone like him?

The answer was obvious…

He had already left.

She looked at that shadowy bubble for a long time before finally dropping her phone back into her purse.

Chapter Fifteen

The next few weeks were difficult. Her father came home, and he was sick. Very sick. April barely had time to think about Nolan, although every so often she'd wake up in the middle of the night, her sex pulsing and wet from dreaming about him. The nights were all she let herself have, though. The rest of her time was devoted to her father's recovery.

One morning four weeks and three days after his last treatment, she took him for his first follow-up exam. The doctor smiled and told them both that although it was early and her dad would still need to come back in three months and then six months for regular tests, it was his opinion that the radiation had been successful, and he was cancer-free. On the way out, April had excused herself to go and cry in the clinic's restroom.

That was the moment she realized that she hadn't actually *heard* what her father had said to her that day in his hospital room, and she hadn't been listening to Nolan when he asked her to help him break down the walls between them.

He'd been offering her something special, and she'd

tossed it back at him as if it wasn't the very thing she needed in her life.

But after spending these hard weeks with her father, confronting the fear that had plagued her for as long as she could remember, she knew without a doubt that taking chances didn't always have to end in loss and pain.

She'd been so wrong. Horribly wrong.

It *wasn't* better to choose loneliness. Loneliness was just another word for emptiness, and she didn't want her life to be empty. She wanted it full of laughter, tears, and passion. If that meant taking some pain and heartbreak along with it, well then, her father had raised her to be strong.

When they got home later that day, Dad was exhausted. He was feeling better every day but still had little stamina and a day like that had taken it all. She helped him settle in on the couch with a blanket. "I think I'll make some soup," she said brightly, turning toward the kitchen.

"April wait," he called.

She went back to his side with a frown. "What is it? Are you uncomfortable?"

"I'm fine." He glanced up and out the front window, looking oddly nervous.

It dawned on her that he was expecting company. She tried to keep a straight face. "So…how's Dory?"

He grinned sheepishly. "Uh, actually, she's coming over with dinner to celebrate my optimistic news."

"Dinner, huh?" She crossed her arms. "Dad, when was the last time you were on a date?"

"With a woman?"

She quirked a brow. "Are we having a different conversation here than I thought?"

He chuckled. "About fifteen years ago."

Her eyes widened. "You haven't even had a *date* since… Mom?"

"Your mother was all I needed for a long time." He hesitated. "I don't want to say that that's changed—"

"You don't have to explain or apologize, Dad," she said gently. He looked abashed, but excited, too. It made him seem more like himself, and she was glad for anything that could keep him looking forward to the future. "You deserve happiness, too."

She hadn't been able to stop thinking about *her* future, about...Nolan. Her father was being blessed with a second chance at life...at love. Why shouldn't they both get one?

She cleared her throat. "I think I'm going to get out of your hair for a while, then." She waved a finger, teasing. "Don't do too much celebrating. It's good that you're feeling better, but you've got a ways to go. I don't want to hear about any wild acrobatics."

He waved his hand. "Yeah, yeah. I'm still your father. Have some respect." He winked. "Besides, she's a nurse. I bet she's an expert at mouth to mouth."

April made a face and laughed. "Ew, okay, that's my cue."

She grabbed her purse from the living room table just as the doorbell rang. She opened it and smiled at the lovely woman on the front stoop dressed in crisp denim and a soft, green silk blouse. "Hi Dory, nice to see you again. You look wonderful," she said, stepping back to let the woman in, then closing the door. "Although the hospital scrubs have a kind of flair you just can't get anywhere else."

"Especially those lovely printed ones they wear in Pediatrics with the puppies and cartoons on them. I keep telling the administration that we should put on a fashion show for the patients." She laughed, a tinkling sound that made April even happier for her father.

April grabbed her jacket, and Dory's smile faded. "I didn't mean to run you out of your home," she said. "Why don't you have dinner with us?" She lifted the grocery bag in her hand.

"I've brought plenty for everyone."

"No, but thanks for the offer. You guys have fun. I think I'll take this opportunity to… There's someone I have to see, before it's too late." Hopefully it wasn't *already* too late.

She started to leave, but stopped short and looked back at her father, who hadn't gotten up from the couch.

Dory touched her arm. "He'll be fine," she said softly.

April nodded. "You know, I think you're right."

She opened the door, only to stop short as she almost walked into the fist raised to knock—at eye-level with her forehead.

"Nolan!" Her heart leaped.

As often as he'd been in her dreams these last weeks, she would have thought it'd be easier to come face to face with him. But her heart started pounding so loud she could hear it, and her breathing hollowed out. His arm still hung between them. She tipped her head to look around it and caught her breath.

He seemed bigger than she remembered, smoother, and more intense. Something else about him had changed, and it was subtle but immediately noticeable. It was in the tight set of his shoulders and the focused look he leveled on her, so different from the laid-back playboy she'd been sent to protect what felt like eons ago.

Serious. Steve Nolan was standing on her porch, completely and utterly serious.

The front door quietly clicked closed behind her, and she realized that the entire world had shrunk the moment he'd arrived.

He still hadn't said anything…and she was too nervous to say anything. Why had he come? Was this her second chance? What if she screwed it up again? What if he *left* again?

"What are you doing here?" she finally asked, her voice cracking.

"I tried to give you some space." He stepped closer. "I heard from your boss at the security company that you were taking time off to be with your father, and I didn't want to get in the way of that."

She swallowed. "I picked up the phone a thousand times," she blurted out. "But after what happened in the hospital, I thought…I thought you were done for good."

"For about five minutes, I thought the same thing. I told myself I'd never needed to chase after any woman, especially one who wasn't willing to share herself with me, who wasn't ready to make *me* a priority." He grimaced. "But it only took one night without you to admit how fucking selfish that was. I put up just as many walls between us as you did."

"What changed?" she whispered, her cheeks hot.

"I remembered that I never give up on something I want."

She held her breath. Could she risk the pain that might eventually come with losing him?

"I want *you*, April."

She hesitated. "Now that my dad's doing better, I've decided to reapply to the FBI training program. If I'm successful, I would be going back to Quantico to complete my training and then…"

He didn't miss a beat. "That's fantastic news, both about your dad and about your training." He sounded absolutely sincere. "But it doesn't change a thing between us."

"What do you mean? How would that work? We'd never see each other."

"I suppose you haven't been keeping up with the business section the last few weeks?"

She frowned. "Not really." Helping her father had become her sole focus, and she'd buried herself in it because it had also kept her mind off Nolan and all the things she should have told him to keep him from walking out the last time. She tried to remember those things now, but all she could think was *Don't go, don't go, don't go.*

"Without any stalkers or threats against me and the company to make our stockholders uneasy, Harrison and I were able to close our big deal this week." His eyes glowed with boyish excitement. "And the first thing I did was pick up the phone to call you, because *you* were the one I needed to share it with."

"Me?"

He let out an exasperated groan. "April Porter, you're the one I want to share it *all* with. Successes, failures, ideas, and plans for the future. All of it. How the hell can you not get that, yet?"

"Maybe because you never told me?"

"I told you in a hundred different ways," he said, stepping even closer. He reached up and slipped his hand behind the nape of her neck. He kissed her with such burning intensity, she might be able to breathe fire when he pulled away. "It was in every touch, every look, and every kiss."

She pressed her fingers to her lips, joy and hope blooming. But she had to be sure this was more than just Nolan deciding he wasn't done with the challenge of her. "You've never had a relationship that lasted longer than five minutes in your entire life. Remember when I asked you if you wanted one? Well, you didn't say yes."

"You're right." He paused. "Neither did you."

"You were right when you said someone had hurt me," she blurted. "His name was Jeremy, and we dated for six months. Then I went to a fancy party with him like the one you took me to, and I overheard him telling his friends that he was just seeing how the other half lived, but he was done with slumming and it was time to get serious…with someone more suitable to his social position and who would fit in with his future goal of becoming governor."

"What a fuckwit," Steve snarled. "Just wait until he tries

to run for office. I'll make sure everyone knows what a selfish, pompous little douchebag he is."

"He said…" She paused, having difficulty getting the words out. She couldn't remember the last time she'd shown this much emotion to anyone other than her father. "He said a lot of the same things I overheard your mother say when I was hiding in the bedroom of your apartment that morning."

He swore and took her hand. "My mother didn't mean it that way. Well, she did, but…she thinks that reclaiming our past life will somehow make up for everything that our father cost us." He pulled her closer, and she bit her lip as part of her tumbled into the gold flecks sparkling in his eyes.

"But she really only wants us all to be happy, and you make me feel more alive, more successful, more worthy than a hundred of those empty society girls, because with you I'm real." His tone was raw; there was none of the teasing playboy left in him. For once, he was showing her exactly who he was, exactly what he felt. "When she sees that, she'll come around."

April swallowed hard. "It doesn't matter. You were right when you called me a coward. I opened myself up before and lost, so how can I bet everything on you now? How do I know it's going to stick, and that you won't be looking for the next best thing in a couple of months, or a year?"

He shook his head. "You don't, and if you're looking for a guarantee, the only one thing I can give you is my promise to always be open with you." His gaze narrowed. "But I'm going to need the same promise from you, because that's the only way we're going to make it work."

He took another step forward so that she had to look up to hold on to his gaze. "Can you do that? Can you love me despite my track record and my past?" he murmured gently, smoothing his thumb across her cheek. "Can you forget about where you *think* you belong and embrace a world where we can be in gym shorts in a boxing ring one minute, and dressed up at a gala event the next?"

His tone was teasing, but it was no longer a game he played with her, or a mask that he wore. His real self showed through in the emotion pouring from his gaze, warming her from the inside out.

Her mouth was dry and her nerves jangled, but it wasn't from fear or uncertainty. Love and hope filled her to overflowing. "Only if you can love me despite my prickly pride and ugly suits." She grinned. "And as long as that world is right here, right now."

He ran his hand over her hair tenderly, before tipping her chin up and claiming her mouth.

"*I* am here," he murmured against her lips, leaving her breathless and whole as a tidal wave of love washed over her with his words. "Right here. Right now."

"Then let's do this," she whispered.

His chuckle rumbled all the way through her. "That's my brave Amazon warrior."

Acknowledgments

First and foremost, my husband and son always go above and beyond to accommodate my crazy schedule. Thank you both for feeding me occasionally and patting my head when I moan out loud.

I wish to thank my agent Courtney Miller-Callihan, who has become someone on whom I rely for her wisdom, advice, and guidance, even though I try not to bombard her with emails and insanity.

This book took many forms before arriving at the story it is today, but my amazing critique partners Christine, Kim, Paula, and Amy helped me – as they do with every book – to sharpen my focus and stay on track. For them I am always supremely grateful.

But as with every book, it is the editing that puts the pretty shine on a finished story, and Tracy Montoya's insight was absolutely invaluable. Thank you, thank you, thank you for all that you do.

About the Author

J.K. Coi is a multi-published, award-winning author of contemporary and paranormal romance and urban fantasy. She makes her home in Ontario, Canada, with her husband and son and a feisty black cat who is the uncontested head of the household. While she spends her days immersed in the litigious world of insurance law, she is very happy to spend her nights writing dark and sexy characters who leap off the page and into readers' hearts.

Find her online at www.jkcoi.com, and visit her alter ego, Chloe Jacobs, who writes thrilling dark fantasy for young adults, at www.chloejacobs.com.

HER SWORN ENEMY
a Men of the Zodiac novel by Theresa Meyers

Headstrong antiquities expert Belladonna Dupre has put every asset she has into recovering her family's fortunes from a shipwreck in the Gulf of Mexico. Problem is she needs a dive salvage operator to make it happen. Enter black sheep of the McCormack dynasty, Tucker McCormack. He wants to give his autocratic, wealthy family the finger, and prove once and for all that he's a self-made man. But when he demands joint credit for the discovery and Bella won't back down, it'll be a battle on the high seas.

BAITING THE BOSS
a novel by Coleen Kwan

For years Grace Owens harbored a secret crush on her boss, Jack Macintyre. But after tragedy upends his life, Jack relocates to a remote tropical island, cutting off all contact with his past. Now Grace's new boss issues an ultimatum: return Jack to the family fold or pack her briefcase and move on. When Grace turns up at Jack's bungalow, he lets her bait him with temptation. Will Jack give up his island paradise to help Grace keep her job? If he stays, she'll lose her job. But if he goes, she'll lose her heart.

i

www.ingramcontent.com/pod-product-compliance
Lightning Source LLC
Chambersburg PA
CBHW031954240626
47153CB00003B/986